MONTGOMERY'S REVENGE

THE HALF-BREED GUNSLINGER III

BRET LEE HART

Montgomery's Revenge
    The Half-Breed Gunslinger III
Copyright 2013, 2022 Bret Lee Hart
ISBN-13: 9798822110861
Cover Art Copyright 2022 Laura Shinn Designs
http://laurashinn.yolasite.com
(Revised cover & formatting, 2022)

Montgomery's Revenge is a work of fiction. Though actual locations may be mentioned, they are used in a fictitious manner and the events and occurrences were invented in the mind and imagination of the author except for the inclusion of actual historical facts. Similarities of characters or names used within to any person – past, present, or future – are coincidental except where actual historical characters are purposely interwoven.

MONTGOMERY'S REVENGE
The Half-Breed Gunslinger III

Duke Montgomery is an Indian fighter – a hard-as-nails killer, plain and simple – who doesn't think twice about ambushing a man or killing him face-to-face. When he learns his brother Richard is dead, killed by the Half-Breed Gunslinger, Duke goes on the hunt.

To avoid trouble after his dealings with Richard Montgomery, Hunter James Dolin and the woman, Helen, travel deep into the Everglades to live in peace for a while. But, as is the way of the world, trouble soon comes looking for them.

How many will die as Montgomery seeks the Half-Breed Gunslinger to get revenge? And what surprises are in store for Hunter James Dolin?

CHAPTER ONE

North Texas, 1864

Adobe Walls was a trading post located in the panhandle of northern Texas, a founding for buffalo hunters, Indian fighters, and frontiersmen from all across the fruited plain. The brick structure was a large, single-entrance fort with walls that rose nine feet high, built to thwart Indian attacks from the Comanche, the Kiowa, and the plains Apache. Buffalo hides, Indian scalps, and anything else of value were traded by day; drinking, gambling and women were the trade by night. The toughest men in Texas could be found there, competing with one another in every way possible.

One man stood out amongst the rabble; one who had been challenged twice in the early part of his three-month stay at the fort. Those challengers were no more, for the men who tried suffered a horrible death, even for these times. A large stain, left from the blood and guts, could still be seen on the wood planks at the center of the post floor, a reminder to all who crossed the man called Duke. He was well over six feet tall, with a physique that appeared to be chiseled from granite, like a strong man seen in the traveling carnival shows. His head was always freshly shaved bald and he rarely wore a shirt, showing battle scars running across his body like a map of the terrain.

Duke was an Indian fighter and wore a rawhide necklace with a single Indian tooth tied at its center as proof. It was said the tooth was taken from a Comanche Chief, but no one knew for sure and no one dared to quarrel; an Indian scalp hung from his belt seemed to help verify the tale. Two .44 Colt Dragoon revolvers hung from his waist and two twelve-inch Sheffield knives cradled in a crisscross pattern in the front of his belt. Duke was also known for ambushing unsuspected enemies with rifle fire and his double-barrel shotgun; he was a killer, plain and simple, and he enjoyed his work.

Led by a Union Colonel named Christopher 'Kit' Carson, The Battle of Adobe Walls had pushed back the Comanche, the Kiowa, and the plains Apache for a time. The Colonel and his men had been ordered out of the area to help with the final push against the Rebels to the south as the Civil War was winding down to a victory for the north. Duke stayed behind as he 'weren't regular Army and took orders from no one'. He hated the Rebels, but he hated the Indians more and the western plains were still full of savages. Most Indian fighters revered the Comanche as the most powerful Indian Nation of the plains; some said they were the greatest warriors that ever shone under the sun. Duke would not agree; he would say any dumb animal that is cornered fights back and he had many scars to prove it. He knew the Civil War would soon be over and the armies would return to finish wiping out every last Injun from the plains; so he would wait to resume his calling only if his patience would allow.

Duke had access to plenty of money in banks in the Dakotas, as his well-to-do family left him never wanting. Here at the trading post he drank, ate, and fornicated all on tabs he never paid. The last two men who tried him were dead; the former proprietor of the post who was trying to collect a debt, and then the lawman who attempted to arrest him for the killing.

The former Texas Ranger's bloodstain marked the floorboards; his death left the town lawless.

Duke had just beat a giant of a man at arm wrestling at his private table and was gathering up his winnings when one of the working girls sat on his lap and batted her eyes at him. A new gal who would soon realize she made a terrible mistake. Duke grabbed her one-handed by the hair at the nape of her neck and with little effort stood her up by extending his powerful arm. Then without leaving his seat, he released her. With a quick swat, he backhanded the girl across the face, sending her reeling backwards through the room where she crashed into an unoccupied table and some empty chairs. Blood ran from her nose, but the Indian squaw was unaware of her injuries for she lay unconscious, possibly dead.

"What'd you do that fer, Duke?" Slim asked, without raising his voice to this man, while keeping what he thought was a safe distance. He directed two other working girls to remove the young squaw from the area.

"She's lucky her scalp ain't hangin' from my belt," answered Duke, while he shuffled a deck of cards with the speed of a practiced dealer. "Slim, you know I don't fornicate with Injuns. The last thing this world needs is half-breeds running around stinkin'up the place."

"Nobody's gonna pay good money for a beat-up girl."

"What are you gittin' at, Slim? Spit it out and stop wasting my time," Duke pressed, as he glared at the tall skinny man who appeared to be nothing but a sack of bones wearing loose clothing.

Slim spoke very carefully, making sure to keep his hands away from the butt of his gun. "If she dies, I'm out a hundred which I just paid little more than two days ago; and if anything's broke, well, her work's limited."

Duke stood up quickly, leaned out, and with one hand grabbed the skinny man by his shirt. To Slim's surprise, he had misjudged Duke's long reach. With the other hand, Duke snatched up several paper bills from the table and shoved them in Slim's mouth. "Now git, before my patience runs short." Duke shoved the man backward, making him stumble.

Slim pulled the notes from his mouth and scampered from the building before his talk got him in further trouble. He knew if he pushed Duke too hard he would end up with his guts spilled out on the saloon floor from one or both of the razor sharp knives the Indian fighter carried.

Duke sat down and picked the cards up. As he began to shuffle, a boy showed from behind the bar and brought him a new bottle of whiskey then left with the empty. The bald giant ignored the glass and drank straight from the bottle. He lit a cigar, made to look small in his large hands, from a match he struck on the top of the rough wood table.

"You, you, and you," pointed Duke toward several cowboys close by. "Sit; I'm ready to play some cards."

The men sat and put their money on the table while Duke dealt for five-card stud. The crowd in the enormous room had gone back to their business of drinking and gambling after the outbreak Duke caused; some had cleared the building all together.

Duke was smiling again after winning several hands of poker when a courier, marked by the hat he wore, walked through the doors and began to look around the Post. He removed the blue hat with an eagle sewn onto the front and brushed the Texas dust from his front side with it; in his other hand he held a letter.

The courier went to the center of the room and held the paper high; he never noticed he was standing dead center of the large blood and guts spot that stained the wood floor while he spoke. "I have a wire for a Montgomery, a Duke Montgomery, II."

Duke held up the hand that gripped his cards, "Here, over here."

The courier walked to the table and stood before him, the folded paper outstretched.

Duke filled him a shot and then snatched the letter out of his grasp. "Have a drink."

"Thank you, Mister," the courier said, before slamming back the whiskey.

Duke poured him another. "Where's this writing from?" Duke asked as he looked over both sides of the folded note.

"Myakka City, Florida."

"Ah, Richard, my little brother," Duke said with a grin as he opened the one-page letter. As he read, his grin faded into a snarl and his teeth could be heard grinding together from across the room.

The courier and the men at the poker table immediately left the area, sensing danger.

Duke stood with a growl and flipped the heavy wood table over on its face, breaking glasses and knocking over chairs in a flurry of floating cards, paper money, and spinning coins that rolled with a metallic sound. People scampered out of his way as Duke stormed out the doorway of the trading post, never to return.

The saloon tender came around the bar and slid the paper note out from under the backside of a chair; ripped and wet with whiskey, it was still readable.

Myakka City Florida Stop

Richard Montgomery killed at home on Lake Okee-chobee Stop A half-breed Injun Hunter James Dolin said to be murderer Stop Half-breed escaped deep into swamp Stop

♦ ❖ ♦

Duke Montgomery had a new plan and that plan did not include waiting around for the Army to return to Texas. There was plenty of time to slaughter the plains Indians, but for right now, only one Injun interested Duke; the one who killed his little brother.

Duke Montgomery was the firstborn son of James Montgomery, I, making him the II, and his little brother Richard born the III. Their father James Montgomery died many years back from tuberculosis, and Richard now reported to have been murdered. Duke didn't love his father or his brother, for he was incapable of such emotion, but he did know through revenge honor must be restored. A family's honor and strength was important; the word honor had different meanings for different men and Duke Montgomery's unstable mental state was poles apart from most. His idea of honor and strength always revolved around who lived and who died, and by whose hand. In his mind, justice must be done for his little brother, if the reports of his death turned out to be true.

Duke went across the road to the hotel where he lodged and gathered his belongings; He always traveled light, only carrying with him the necessities. On his large buckskin-colored quarter horse, he packed beef jerky, water, whiskey, and extra ammo for his weapons; this included the Dragoon Revolvers, a yellow boy Winchester repeating rifle, and a Stevens ten-gauge, double-barreled shotgun.

Hidden in his bedroll were gold coins and a stash of paper money. It weren't much, but where he was headed, it would go far. Duke could stop at any bank in any city across the country and have access to monies under the Montgomery name.

As an Indian Hunter and fighter, Duke learned to live off the land like an Indian, and he was most comfortable in the wild. Unlike his father and little brother Richard, he had little interest in money unless needed to secure men for killings or to stack chips on the card table. Everything else he needed he would just take, using fear and intimidation backed up with his size and skills, and driven by pure meanness. His methods were simple; kill the leader and anyone else who dared challenge him.

Duke would head out alone to the Florida State; he figured killing one half-Injun should be fairly easy. The man was half-white, which might make him smarter than the normal savage, and he might have friends who would fight by his side, but nothing Duke hadn't handled before. In his younger days, Duke traveled to the Colorado Rockies to fight the children of the Crow that had waged war on a man by making him a legend, a mountain man named Jeremiah Johnson. Johnson had long passed, and Duke engaged the fighting warrior ancestors of the Crow by killing what was left of the diminishing tribe of that area. Duke Montgomery, a legend in his own right, left the Rocky Mountains as one of the greatest Indian killers of his time. Not respected like Johnson, but feared – which was fine by him.

Duke Montgomery left Texas behind and headed south-west for Florida and Myakka City. He would find out the truth of his brother Richard and then brutally kill anyone involved, starting with the half-breed that went by the name Hunter James Dolin.

CHAPTER TWO

Somewhere around a year had passed since Hunter killed Richard Montgomery and his army of red-legs at the big house on the banks of Lake Okeechobee. The half-breed and his woman Helen had left their old friends Walt and Jebidiah behind as the proprietors of the lake house while they moved further south, allowing the winds to guide them. Hunter rode deeper into the swamps, and Helen followed without question. Young and in love for the first time in her life, she knew what she wanted; she just hoped she could convince her man that he wanted it as well.

Hunter had concerns that Montgomery's ties to the northern government and his rich status would bring havoc down on their heads sooner or later, so it would be best for them to fade deep into the swamps like many Seminoles and Miccosukee had over the years. After a time, Hunter found a remote place suitable for them to hole up in solitude; just south of the Everglades, in a swamp called Big Cypress. This swamp was more forgiving than its neighbor as it was higher and dryer than the glades, but it was still a swamp.

Only Indians lived in Big Cypress and any white man who ventured this far south would mysteriously disappear at the hands of the natives. But the Indians kept their distance from the half-breed gunslinger, for he was known to them as *Lus-tee Manito Nak-nee,* which translates to 'Black Spirit Man'. They believed he was possessed by an evil spirit, and if he were killed the evil that dwelled inside him would be released unto the land for a hundred years. The white woman with him was very desirable to the Indian braves, but the leaders forbid them to engage her, for she was said to be under the protection of the half-breed.

Hunter and Helen carved out a plot of land at the edge of a small, secluded lake where they built a hut for shelter; a combination of the Miccosukee's Chickee and the white man's cabin. It was a small one roomer for cover during stormy weather and for sleeping. Mostly they spent their time outdoors hunting, fishing, and cooking on an open fire. The home was built for a short-term stay, as they were just biding their time. Neither mentioned aloud what they were waiting for; in their guts, they somehow knew Hunter would be sought out for the killing of Richard Montgomery and his men.

Walt and Jebidiah were local veterans and, more importantly, they were white men. They would get a pass for their involvement in what was becoming known as the 'Big Lake Massacre'. Justice would have to be served and a half-breed would be the perfect wrongdoer to blame it on.

Hunter tried to convince Helen to move on, to save herself from the grief which would surely come. But she would have none of that talk. Committed to him, for the first time she felt her life had purpose. For the past year, Hunter spent an hour a day teaching her to shoot with a pistol, handle a rifle, and sharpen her skills with a knife, as well as hand-to-hand combat.

Helen carried her own set of pistols Hunter had traded for at a post during their travels between Lake Okeechobee and where they were now, at Big Cypress. The revolvers were .31 caliber five rounds, Baby Dragoons. It was often told that the pocket models were popular with Civil War officers, who did not rely on them as combat arms but rather as defense against battlefield surgeons bent on amputating a limb. They were less powerful and only fired five shots instead of six, making them smaller and lighter, allowing Helen to handle the weapons better. If she could pull them fast and shoot accurately, the weaker calibers would make no difference. They were the perfect size and weight for a gunslinger with a weaker muscular build. With their share of the late Richard Montgomery's stash of gold, Hunter bought as much extra ammo as they could carry, for training practice as well as any confrontation Hunter knew would someday come down the swampy road.

Hunter and Helen had been hiding in the Big Cypress swamp for nearly a year and had done everything they could to prepare. Helen was as fast as most men with her draw and the reloading. Hunter thought she may even be a bit quicker than most. Her aim was as sharp as it was going to get, which was very good; the only question was how steady her nerves would be during battle. Shooting targets was different than killing men, for men were heated and always seemed to shoot back.

Wild game was abundant in these parts and Hunter did not have to travel far to find hog and deer. One day he didn't have to travel at all, when he was surprised by a large black bear attracted to their camp by honeycomb he raided from a beehive. It was a strange battle on that early summer morning as Hunter woke with the sun.

He and his woman slept without clothes, for the heat and humidity of the Florida swamp was always extreme, but they had a rule, always wear your weapons or, at the very least, keep them within arm's reach. Hunter walked outside to relieve himself, and did so wearing nothing but his belt and revolvers. He stood at the edge of the lake with his back to the cabin and stretched. He was in the middle of his bodily task when he heard movement directly behind him.

Hunter began to turn, while pulling his revolver. The black bear quickly lunged, slashing out with his paws, and knocked Hunter into the lake. He was unable to hold onto the pistol as it flew from his hand. It sank to the bottom of the lake and the other pistol was now most likely useless as he went completely under wetting the powder. Hunter came up out of the lake to see the bear headed for the cabin where Helen slept.

Naked, Hunter ran at the bear as he drew the remaining revolver from its holster and pulled the trigger, aiming at the bear's backside. All he got were clicks. The bear had almost reached the cabin door when Hunter caught up with him. He turned the revolver around, using the butt like a club on the backend of the large animal. The bear turned quickly, with a ferocious growl, making Hunter stop and begin stepping backwards.

"*HELEN!!!*" Hunter yelled. "I could use some help out here!"

The bear came at him at a run. Hunter whirled around and ran straight for the lake as fast as he could; after five strides, he dove in. As his head hit the water, he heard gunfire, and then went under. Hunter quickly came back up from the depths, taking a breath of air and turned around, whipping the hair from his eyes as he paddled his feet to stay afloat just off the bottom. A smile of relief and pride came over him at what he saw. Standing naked over the unmoving black bear at the edge of the lake was his beautiful woman, in her hands were two smoking Dragoon revolvers.

"Hell of a mornin'," Helen said, with a big smile.

Hunter left the lake, walked up the bank, and met her by the carcass. He knelt down and laid his hand on the bear's furry back, checking for a heartbeat. She had emptied the guns; three were headshots that had finished the beast off. They would skin and butcher the bear, using every bit of the animal, not wasting any of its resource.

But, first things first; Helen looked stunning to him, her bare hips supporting her gun belt and holsters, and her breasts perfect. Hunter stepped around the dead bear and swept her off her feet. He carried her easily into the cabin, while cradling her in his arms.

The lean bear meat made good steaks and jerky to add to their supplies. From mule deer killed earlier, he had stitched deerskin pouches for water. They gathered mustard root for bullet wounds and coca leaves were ground up for pain. The whiskey bought at the post had long been gone; the empty bottles used to hold Sambucus (elderberry) wine made from the fruit and sugar cane that grew in abundance in the Big Cypress. At all times, Hunter was ready to fight or strike camp and move on in a matter of minutes.

After a year of preparing, the half-breed gunslinger became restless and just plain tired of hiding with the Big Lake Massacre hanging over his head. Helen could feel it too, for she could only be content if so was her man.

Night had fallen and Helen was sleeping deeply in Hunter's arms after their intense lovemaking. Not even the loud song of the whippoorwill that decided to sound off only feet from their cabin could wake her under the warmth of the bearskin blanket.

Hunter was sleeping deeply, but his slumber was not as peaceful, for he was dreaming. His dreams had always guided him in his walk of life, a gift to him from his Indian mother. He always believed her death was for his purpose, to heighten his spiritual senses. Tonight's vision was clearer than they had ever been before.

...he was coming for them on the back of a large quarter horse, a man of great strength, and a limitless evil radiated from his soul. He wore a hat when he rode, but his head appeared to be bare. He had numerous scars covering his face, and his bare arms and chest had the healing marks prominent and protruding on top

of an impressive muscle mass. His legs were long, the size of tree trunks, and the feet and hands were oversized... Hunter began to toss and turn a little in his slumber.

The most dangerous part of this man was his eyes; they had a crazed look about them that seemed familiar...

Hunter woke and sat up quickly, looking around the dark cabin; the whippoorwill sounded off, bringing him back completely from his slumber. It was early morning, about two hours before sun up; Hunter got to his feet and scratched as he walked outside. Time to leave this place and face what was coming for him. The vision was what he was waiting for to guide him to his next move; he could not put all the pieces together, but at least, he now had a direction and an enemy to face.

Helen came out and rested her naked body against his as she wrapped her arms around his waist from behind. Hunter welcomed her touch.

"What is it, my love?" she asked.

"Someone is hunting me."

"Who is it? Who is coming?" She never questioned how he knew the things he knew.

"I don't know exactly; he is far to the north and alone, for now. We must close the gap between him and us; the longer he is on the trail, the more men he will pick up along the way."

Hunter turned and scooped Helen up and into his arms; she laughed and kissed his shoulder as he walked her back inside. Hunter intended to make love to her until the sun came up for he knew when their journey began there would be little time for pleasures on the trail.

They struck the camp with the sun, in a short amount of time, like they planned since the beginning of their stay. They would leave the small cabin standing for any passersby that might need shelter. Hunter knew the Indians would stay away and any white man who stayed here would be protected under the gunslinger's curse.

Hunter rode Zeke, the smartest Appaloosa this side of the Mississippi, Helen rode her Spanish cracker horse, a young and vibrant mare she named 'Girlie'.

"Where are we headed, my man?" asked Helen from her saddle as they began to move forward.

"We ain't took ten steps and already with the questions," Hunter said half-jokingly.

"Hey," replied Helen with a grin, "a girl needs to know, you know."

"Yes, I know," said Hunter with a roll of his eyes. "I think Lake Okeechobee would be a good start, to see some old friends."

"Very good. I had been missin' those two old coots." Helen said with much delight.

Hunter gave Zeke a little kick, the horse took off seeming to enjoy being back on the trail. Helen reacted and tucked her mare to the Appaloosa's tail. They left the place they had called home for the last eight months, never to return.

Chapter Three

Duke Montgomery traveled southwest along the Oklahoma-Texas border, skimming Arkansas, and then into central Louisiana where he turned more to the west, and into Mississippi. He sidestepped towns and posts, for the most part, living off the land. Duke only avoided confrontation so it would not slow him down, for he rather enjoyed conflict with men, his anger always looming below the surface. Now he had the need for revenge fueling him.

A month and some weeks of travel had left his tobacco and whiskey supplies dangerously low, and it was time for a night in town. He began searching for signs of paths and roadways which would eventually lead him to what would pass as civilization in this backwoods state. Duke hated the south and he hated southerners, he was a Yankee through and through.

He finally found a path that led to a road which he followed, only stopping when he came along a crude wooden sign that simply read, *Chimney Ville*. There were marks of war all along Duke's travels, especially heavy on the road he now traveled. He turned the quarter horse at the sign and made his way for about a half-mile, until he entered the town. Duke could see why the town had been named Chimney Ville, for only the chimneys of most of the homes were left standing.

Duke rode his horse at a walk through the settlement, sitting high in the saddle. He sensed he was being watched from many of the dilapidated buildings.

When he reached the center of the town, he stopped in front of the newly rebuilt saloon with a hotel next to a half-built feed store. Duke jerked his head quickly, his hand going to the butt of his revolver, as a bang rang out from behind him, many bangs followed. He relaxed. Several Negroes wearing Union garb carried lumber and hammered wood planks into place, rebuilding the feed store.

Dismounting, Duke tied the horse to a post and entered the saloon through the swinging doors. There was a long bar to his left and chairs and tables to his right. As his eyes adjusted to the dim room, he could see men drinking and playing cards at several of the tables. Two other men were at the far end of the bar; most looked in his direction as he entered. Duke stood just inside the door and stared down every man in the room one at a time, giving them each a chance to say something or make a move. There were no challengers; the men went back to their business as the huge, bald stranger found his spot at the end of the bar.

"What'll you have?" asked the portly bartender.

"Whiskey and a beer," replied Duke as he flipped a gold piece onto the counter. He would pay for this round since he had not decided how long he might stay in this place.

The man behind the bar filled the shot glass and left the bottle. Duke slammed it back and poured himself another; he downed the second one then filled it again. The bartender returned with his mug of beer.

"There's meat at the hotel, women too. The girls come in here later in the day; it's a little early yet."

Duke glared into the eyes of the man over the top of his beer as if to say 'I didn't ask'. The bartender walked away, sensing danger. Duke sized up the men in the saloon further while he struck a match and lit a cigar. The ones at the tables were seasoned Union soldiers, dressed all in blue. But the two at the far end of the bar were younger, also in blue, but with one difference;

they wore red leather chaps over their boots. Their curiosity kept them staring toward the large, shirtless man.

Finally, Duke spoke, "If you two are gonna' keep eye-ballin' me, you best come buy me a drink to fill my bladder so's I can piss on your graves."

The two men looked at one another with doubt at first, but then they knew they must confront this man for their honor's sake. The young red legs walked down to Duke's end of the bar. He stood at the corner making it easy for them to converse face to face. One man brought along his bottle and filled the bald, muscled man's glass to the rim.

Duke slammed the shot back and held it out for another. The man looked at his partner who nodded in agreement, so he filled the glass once again. Duke did not thank them, for manners were not one of his strong points; he considered them a waste of his time.

"Red-legs, huh?" said Duke. "Who you ridin' with?"

"We were with Captain Terrill and his Jayhawkers out of Kansas and Missoura," said one.

"Were?" Duke asked.

The other man picked up where the first one left off. "They left us here with them regulars." The man pointed over his shoulder with his thumb toward the soldiers at the table. "In case the rebels double back and try to take back the town."

Duke blew black smoke from his nostrils and said, "The Rebels ain't comin' back here anytime soon."

"How do you know that, mister?" asked one.

"Cuz I seen 'em, a sizable battalion of Gray riders headed for Texas, Terrill and his red-legs were on their trail, about two days behind." Duke smoked his cigar and drank his beer, allowing this new information to sink into the small minds of the two men. He waited quietly as they conversed.

"That's just great, Billy. Means we're stuck here and runnin' outta money fast."

"Shut up, Junior. I'm tryin' to think on it."

Billy was slightly older than his partner who went by the name Junior, and seemingly, Billy was the brains of their two-man outfit.

"Where you headed, mister?" asked Billy.

"Myakka City is my first stop," replied Duke.

"Where's that at, Billy?" whispered Junior, leaning toward Billy.

"Not sure," said Billy, "Where's that city at, Mister? Maybe we could tag along with yah?"

There it was; Duke had just recruited these two easily with his larger mind. He grabbed the whiskey bottle by its neck, and with the other hand chugged the last of his beer then slammed the glass mug on the counter. "We leave tomorrow mornin' at sunup, meet me at the hotel. You will be paid if you do your jobs and don't git yourself killed." Duke turned and headed for the door, taking his whiskey bottle with him.

"What might our jobs be?" said Billy to his back.

The shirtless, scarred, muscle man stopped and turned after two steps. "We're going to Florida to kill a stinkin' half-breed."

Billy and Junior looked at one another and grinned with confidence that the job would be easy enough.

"What do your friends call you, Mister?" Junior asked.

"I don't have any friends, but you will call me Sir." Duke turned and walked out, leaving the saloon doors swinging behind him.

The red-legs at the bar smugly drank their bottle, happy they were getting out of this desolate town; they were hoping to make some real money for a change. The Army owed them three months back pay, but they knew it would be hard pressed to get. How hard could it be to kill one half-Injun anyway? One look at Duke told them this guy needed help from no one, but if he was willing to pay for some back-up killers? That would be fine by them, with that they had no problem.

One of the veteran soldiers from the table walked up to the bar next to Billy and ordered a beer from the bartender.

"Seen you talkin' with the bald man, Billy. Goin' somewhere's?" asked the soldier.

"That's none a' your concern, Major," answered Billy.

The bartender returned with the beer, the two men stopped talking, and all three made eye contact. The Major tossed a coin on the bar and waited for the barkeep to walk away before he continued with the talk. "As your temporary commanding officer, it is my concern, and abandoning your post is a hangin' offense."

Hearing this, Junior turned around with his back to the bar and rested one palm on the butt of his gun, keeping an eye on the soldiers at their back.

"Don't threaten us, Major," growled Billy. "We're Jayhawkers and answer only to Captain Terrell, and no one else."

"Yeah, we could quarrel on that," said the Major in a calm but forceful voice. "But you know what, red-leg? I don't give a shit. You two are soldiers without honor and I don't like you around my men. So, you have a nice trip – I won't stand in your path."

The Union Major went back to his men at the table who had been on high alert since Junior turned toward them. Billy smiled at the Major and there was a moment of tension, until Billy lightly smacked Junior on the chest. Then they backed out of the saloon, not once taking their eyes off the Major or his men.

"We gonna' let 'em go, Major?" asked a soldier at the table.

"I got no use for red-legs," said the Major as he began shuffling a deck of cards. "You know who that bald ruffian was at the bar they were talking to?"

The men at the table looked at one another, some shook their heads no.

"That's Duke Montgomery."

"The Indian fighter?" questioned another of the men.

"The very same, all the evil that make up men is all rolled up in that massive body, but the biggest danger is in that bald head of his. Worse than any red-leg, and when Montgomery is done with them two, he'll cut their throats without pause and leave them to the worms."

The soldiers at the table broke out in laughter and continued with their card game, not giving it another thought.

Billy and Junior packed up their belongings and went to the hotel where the bald man was staying. They tied their steeds to the hitching post and went to sleep on the front porch.

The hotel proprietor spotted them through the window and went to remove them. When he walked outside and saw the red leather coverings on the legs of the men, he decided to leave them be. The owner would not sleep tonight with Montgomery upstairs and the red-legs sleeping on his front stoop. His nerves would be on edge until they moved on from his hotel, and hopefully out of Mississippi altogether.

Chapter Four

Hunter and Helen traveled for two days, heading north through the Big Cypress swamp, and they entered the Everglades in the hours of mid-morn. The Indians of Big Cypress had been seen shadowing them from a distance, time to time, since they left the cabin. Hunter figured they wanted to know where his evil spirits were leading him. The Seminoles had watched his and Helen's every movement since they'd lived in the cabin, and now they were on the move, the Indians followed.

The swampy path they traveled was narrow for a time, and then the trail suddenly changed, opening up into a large clearing on higher ground. The mound was made up of limestone and a small forest of pine trees grew around the edge. Hunter brought Zeke to a halt, "Whoa, boy." Helen stopped Girlie alongside him. Nothing was said for a moment as Hunter surveyed the area, the only sounds the buzz of the crickets and swamp bugs coming from the foggy tree line. Hunter looked to the sky to see two bald eagles circling overhead.

"Hunter, what is it?" Helen finally asked with a whisper.

"This is sacred Indian land; we should go around this clearing."

"What will happen if we don't?" asked Helen.

"I don't know," replied the gunslinger.

Before they could change direction, the buzzing sounds of the insects suddenly stopped. The woods became eerily silent. Hunter put his hand on the butt of his revolver, Helen did the same.

Out of the trees, like ghosts in the night, appeared Indians through the mist – some on horseback, others on foot. They walked toward him and Helen and encircled them from the front. Hunter looked to his back to see braves coming up the trail cutting off any retreat.

"Easy, Helen," directed Hunter quietly. "Keep them Dragoons holstered, but slowly cock the hammers and keep your hands on both of 'em, put the reins in your teeth."

Helen did as she was told; the click of the hammers could be heard by all as the Indians moved in on them. The Injuns continued slowly, until they were about five horse lengths away, and then stopped. Hunter looped his reins around the saddle horn, then pulled both Colts, spun them forward and then backward, then side to side, in an impressive display of speed and skill for all to see. He then re-holstered the .44s, leaving the hammers cocked. The Indians made no movement as they kept their rifles and loaded bows at the ready, but didn't take any action.

Several braves in front of the gunslinger parted, allowing their Chief to enter the circle on an Appaloosa that looked a lot like Zeke. Its blotchy patterns were different, but the colors were the same and located similarly at the hindquarters.

Hunter recognized the Chief and a glimmer of hope flashed across his mind.

"*Lus-tee Manito Nak-nee*, Hunter James Dolin," said the Chief, "I am Apayaka Hadjo, Chief of the Miccosukee."

"Yes," spoke Hunter. "The white man calls you Sam Jones. I remember us meeting in a way not much different than this," Hunter took his left hand off his revolver and fanned out his arm pointing out their surroundings, "not too long ago."

"Yes," said the Chief. "I sense your black heart has healed much, your bad spirit is weak, less dangerous to my people."

"Make no mistake, Sam Jones," Hunter stared the Chief down with his steel blue eyes, "I am more dangerous now than ever and willing to die here with you, if I must."

There was a long pause as the two men stared at one another. It was the Chief's move, for he had the upper hand. Helen still had her palms resting on her gun butts, and the taste of bitter leather began to overwhelm her as she bit down on the reins in her mouth.

"You have wandered onto sacred Miccosukee land, there must be punishment."

"The only punishment, Chief, will be my death and yours, which I can promise," replied Hunter sternly. "Seminole blood runs through my veins, I do know that payment could settle this, if you would allow it."

The Chief seemed to be pondering this over in his mind before he spoke. "You may go, Gunslinger; leave the white woman for payment."

Helen's eyes opened wide as she looked from the Chief to Hunter, the reins still dangling from her teeth.

"Chief, your braves don't want this white woman," spoke Hunter with a grin. "Yes, she does keep one warm during cold nights, but she never stops talking, *yap, yap, yap.*" Hunter made a gesture by opening and closing his hand like the mouth of a puppet, "Like the chi Wawa, *yap, yap yap.*"

Sam Jones and most of the warriors who understood broke out with laughter.

Helen looked around, not believing what she was hearing.

The Chief pointed at Helen. "Her Indian name will be Leathers In Mouth." Sam Jones and the braves broke out with more laughter, even louder than before.

Helen looked to Hunter, who was laughing right along with them; she spit the reins from her teeth with disgust and tensed up on her pistol butts. Hunter gave her a look that said, *Don't do it.* She was so angry right then, it took everything she had not to shoot every one of these men. As the laughter died down, Helen removed her hands from her guns and crossed her arms in disgust. Some of the braves talked amongst one another, obviously making fun of her.

Hunter quickly began to barter with the Chief; he pulled a bottle of elderberry wine from his saddlebag, along with a pouch of tobacco. He rode closer to the Chief and handed the pouch over to him, and then he handed him the wine.

"This will keep you warm tonight without the yap." Hunter dared not look back to Helen, for he knew he would pay for that comment for some time.

The Chief popped the cork, smelled the mouth of the bottle, and then took a sip. He smiled as the liquid burned, but at the same time was sweet. Hunter could see that the Chief was close to a decision. Without pause, he pulled out another bottle of wine and handed it to Sam Jones; the Indian smiled big.

The Chief pulled a tomahawk from his waist belt and handed it to Hunter. The gunslinger noticed for the first time that Sam Jones had extremely long and powerful-looking arms. He hoped he would not have to fight this man. Hunter held the tomahawk in his hand by its wooden handle; it was well balanced and the head was made of steel, the double edges were razor sharp as Hunter ran his thumb across the blade.

"It has killed many white men," the Chief boasted.

"It is a fine weapon, and I will be honored to kill with it," Hunter said, as he slid it into his belt, crisscrossing it with his thirteen-inch Bowie knife. The tension in the air passed as the braves withdrew into the trees; Chief Apayaka Hadjo of the Miccosukee tribe stayed behind and stared at Hunter for some time.

At last he spoke, "I have seen a vision through the Spirit that told me to bring you this weapon. Take heed of the bald man who was born with the evil soul. *Lustee Manito Nak-nee* you must be again, if you are to defeat this evil." The chief turned his horse and headed for the tree line. "Fight well, half-breed, and perhaps we will meet again?" And then, he was gone.

"I reckin' so, Chief, I reckin' we just might at that," Hunter replied quietly.

Hunter could feel Helen's eyes burning a hole in the back of his head. He suddenly wished the Indians had not left him alone with her, and he had an urge to follow them into the woodlands.

"Don't be upset," said Hunter as he turned to face Helen. "It is what I had to do."

She said nothing; she just stared away from him with her arms crossed.

"Let's go." Hunter steered Zeke across the raised clearing and back to the path that began once more at the other side. He did not look back, but he could sense Helen following behind him.

They traveled quietly for the rest of the day without stopping for a mid-day meal, eating jerky while in the saddle. They did not speak; Hunter enjoyed the silence for a time, but then it seemed to become a little silly. He looked back to her several times. She pretended to be looking somewhere else, down to the ground, up into the sky, once she caressed the mane of her horse. *That is one stubborn woman,* thought Hunter, as he rolled his eyes upward and looked to the sky.

The sun's movement seemed to speed up as it drew closer to the horizon and approached late afternoon. For the last hour, Hunter could smell an odor in the breeze that he had been searching for. As the land changed, so did the air, the swamp had a certain smell. A pine forest or the mangroves growing by an ocean could be identified by their individual odors, and the scent he smelled in the air was certain. They rode out of the tree-line and the breeze off what the Seminoles call 'the Big Lake' hit them like a hammer; Lake Okeechobee was massive.

An Osprey chirped from a branch that showed signs of a lightning strike at the top of a dead pine tree just off the shore. Hunter recalled seeing this tree where he once fished for a meal. He figured they were now a day and a half's ride from the stilt house where their old friends Jebidiah and Walt had settled.

"We'll camp here for the night," said Hunter. There was no answer from Helen; the silent treatment was in full effect.

They dismounted next to some downed oak logs, just off the bank of the lake; then removed the saddles from Zeke and Girlie, for a much needed rest.

"I'll fetch some wood for a fire," Hunter said, again without any reply from Helen. "Stay on your guard, I don't sense no-one around, but you can't be too wary." *Okay, Hun?* Hunter thought, as he took to the brush for the gathering of the firewood. The half-breed spoke quietly to himself as he picked up dead wood, "What else could I do? The Indian don't see women as equals, they see them as weak."

Hunter had as much wood as he could carry so he headed back to camp. He suddenly stopped in his tracks as something dawned on him, some of his thoughts spoken aloud, *"Women may not be physically strong as men,* but she's got me talking to myself like a fool – there's power there."

He shook his head and continued on, determined to break down this ridiculous wall she had built between them. He was the man and he would put his foot down; and then apologize. If that didn't work, he would have to come up with something else.

The silent treatment continued as he built the fire and brewed coffee. Helen sat in front of the flames nibbling on a piece of jerky, totally ignoring him. Hunter pulled the last bottle of Elderberry wine from the saddlebag that rested on the oak log; he then walked over to Helen and sat down next to her. She did not move away, but stopped chewing for a moment, and then continued eating again, staring into the fire. Hunter took a swig and then offered the bottle to her. She ignored it, only looking forward.

"Helen, please, I had to play along."

She turned and looked at him for the first time in a while. "I understand that," Helen replied, disapproval in her voice, "but you seemed to enjoy it way too much."

Hunter could not help but laugh, which caught her off guard 'cause the half-breed didn't laugh often. "No, no, I was bluffin'; please tell me how I can make it up to you."

"I don't know, but you better think of somethin'."

Hunter looked around thinking hard, when he thought he spotted a possible way out. He stood up and handed Helen the bottle, "Here hold this."

She took it and watched him walk toward the lake while unbuckling his guns. He dropped them to the ground as he went and, to her surprise, he didn't stop at the water's edge but kept on 'til he was waist deep, boots and all. A smile grew across her face as he turned and walked out of the lake. He held a beautiful white flower that grew from the lily pads which covered sections of Lake Okeechobee.

He stood over her and handed her the dripping wet flower. She accepted it from him with a growing smile, then she broke out with laughter. As he sat down by her side, water poured from his boots, making him laugh too.

With a groan, he grabbed her and pulled her on top of him. She screamed as she felt the cold water from his wet clothes soaking into hers. He took the bottle of wine from her loose grasp, saving it from hitting the dirt as she kissed him hard on the lips. Hunter leaned back against the oak log and pulled her close. She snuggled into his chest while admiring the flower.

"All right, Mister, you're forgiven," said Helen. "But if any man or Injun talks to me like that again, they will see what a trained woman can do with two loaded Colt Dragoons."

"I have no doubt, woman, I have no doubt." Hunter took a swig of the wine. "We should reach the big house in two days. I hope Jebidiah and Walt has whiskey, or somethin' stronger."

"Have you ever known them not to be holdin' liquor?" asked Helen. She then brought the flower to her nose and smelled the aroma of her lily.

"You're right once again, my lady. If they are still there, they will have something stronger than wine, that's fer sure."

The trusted whippoorwill began to sing its song like clockwork as the sun went down. Helen had drifted off to sleep, leaving the gunslinger alone with his thoughts. He made mental notes to himself as he glanced over to his pistol belt that lay on the ground and out of reach. He didn't wish to move, with Helen asleep and comfortable in his arms, but it was important to know where their weapons were. She was wearing her guns. He could pull one pistol easily as it stuck out on her curvy hip.

The whippoorwill continued its constant song as Hunter began to drift off. The Native Indians believed the singing of this bird was a death omen. Hunter wasn't sure he believed this. It was his last thought before sleep overcame him.

CHAPTER FIVE

"Where the hell is we, Billy?" Junior asked from his saddle at the rear of the three-man line.

"Shut up, Junior." Billy replied from just in front of Junior.

The bald Montgomery was leading the way at a distance of three and sometimes five or more horse lengths ahead. Duke always pushed hard and the young red legs sometimes had a tough time keeping up with his pace.

"Well, when is we gonna' get there? We're almost outta' whiskey, and we been sleepin' in the dirt for a week now."

Duke was far ahead of them as Billy purposely slowed down their pace when Junior began complaining again, so not to irritate Montgomery. But Duke's hearing was sharp, and he turned his oversized quarter horse around and closed the distance.

Billy and Junior stopped their animals as he came forward; they immediately went on their guard as fear crept up their backside.

In a surprisingly calm voice, Duke spoke, "I can see why your commander left you two idiots behind."

The men said nothing, just took it like children being scolded by their father.

"My map tells me we're close to the Alabama, Florida border. I want you two to shut your traps and keep a watchful eye from here on out. There should be a town up ahead and a saloon. No better place to git information than a saloon."

"Yes Sir, Mr. Montgomery, Sir," replied Billy.

Junior said this also, his voice breaking just a bit.

Duke stared them down for a moment, and then he turned his horse back around and headed forward. They traveled along the path for a time, stopping when the land opened up into a clearing. A town stood in the center of a small hilly valley, a wooden sign off to their left read *TALLAHASSEE*.

Junior tried to read it, sounding the letters out slowly, "Tall-a-hay-see?"

Duke jerked his head toward the young man, a disgusted look on his face. "Tallahassee, stupid!"

"That's a dumb name." said Junior, trying to justify his ignorance.

"It's an old Muskogee Indian word, Creek, or maybe Seminole. Don't matter which, for they're all the damn same. Tallahassee translates to 'Old fields'," Duke explained.

"Don't make much sense to me," pronounced Billy as he tried to help cover for Junior, like he had most of their time together.

"For some reason," continued Duke, "politicians are compelled to name lands after the Injuns that they just stole it from, after they slaughter 'em or run them on to reservations. Personally," smiled Duke, "the only good Indian is a dead Indian."

Both Billy and Junior grinned along with their new commander.

"Wipe that grin off your faces," Montgomery barked as his demeanor suddenly changed, "I hear the Union has taken this capital city, but that don't mean there ain't bushwhackers around, so be on alert."

Duke turned his horse and headed down the hill, the red-legs tucked in behind him as they rode toward the city. After a while, they found the dirt road that led into the town that looked to be at least two miles long.

There were small farms on the outskirts with pens holding milking cows, pigs, and chickens.

Men, women, and children stopped their chores and stared at the three men as they slowly rode by, the look of dislike clear on their faces. The tension in the air felt so thick it could be cut with a knife. Duke Montgomery was a sight to behold, but it was the blue uniforms with the red leg coverings on Billy and Junior that the southerners knew well.

After a while, small wooden farmhouses turned to larger, fancier plantation style mansions behind rod iron gates. A company of four union soldiers appeared, on foot walking down the road toward them, with two shackled uniformed rebels at the center of the line. Montgomery, Billy, and Junior were riding nose to tail down the middle of the two lane road forcing the soldiers to move to the side as they passed one another.

The blue shirts gave them a dirty look, but said nothing. The soldiers veered off the road and forced the prisoners down with a shove into a small dry ditch. The rebels got back to their feet and stood proudly while facing their accusers; then, shots rang out.

Duke and the boys came to an abrupt halt, turning quickly to see the prisoners in grey fall to the ground dead.

"I think it's very clear who's runnin' this town," commented Billy. "Shit!" Billy realized his hand was on the butt of his revolver and his thumb had cocked the hammer. He released it and relaxed a bit as the soldiers pulled out shovels and began to throw dirt on top of the men, they didn't seem to mind that one of the rebels was still moving, clearly still alive.

Duke, Billy, and Junior continued on 'til they reached the busy streets in front of a large hotel, eatery, and saloon. They tethered their horses to one of the several hitching posts and dismounted.

Duke spoke quietly to Billy and Junior, "I'm goin' in first, wait 'til the count of ten, and then come in behind me. Keep your distance and watch my back, got it?"

They nodded their heads in agreement.

Duke took the three steps and entered through the saloon's swinging doors. He stopped just inside and looked around. Men looked back at him, and then some returned to their business of eating, drinking, and card playing. Some conversed with one another at the sight of this wide, shirtless man with the scarred body and a height that towered over most.

Duke's spurs clanked on the wood-planked floor as he walked up to an opening at the corner of the bar. A heavy red head, with her cleavage bursting from her dress, came alongside of him.

"Can I git you some of this, Mister?"

Duke glanced at her upper body as she stirred her shoulders back and forth and fluttered her eyes at him with a smile. When he lifted his head, their eyes met under the brim of his hat, and the smile on her face faded as she suddenly felt she was in grave danger.

"Move along, whore. I don't have time for you right now," Duke warned.

The woman backed away slowly and bumped into several people in her haste to get away.

The bartender spoke, bringing duke's head back around. "What'll you have?"

"Whiskey."

The barkeep was an older man, nicely dressed, with a handlebar mustache. He popped the cork and poured the shot glass full.

Duke slapped a coin on the bar top and said, "You look like a man that is full of information?"

"Maybe I see and hear a few things, from time to time," the bartender replied.

Montgomery slapped two more gold coins on the bar and slid them toward the man. A roar came from the far corner of the saloon as a brawl broke out, seemingly from a card game, and Duke jerked his head around. As he did, he spotted Billy and Junior sitting at a table as a woman set down two glasses and a bucket of brewed chuck. Duke emptied his shot glass with a tip of his head and slammed it on the bar; the bartender was quick to fill it.

"I'm looking for a half-breed." Duke said plainly.

"Lots of half-breeds around," said the server, as he wiped out beer mugs with a dirty rag. "Florida is a melting pot; you got Injuns, Negroes, Crackers, and nowadays you got blue coats and red legs from the north – like I said a melting pot."

"I'm lookin' for a particular half-breed, one named Hunter James Dolin."

The man behind the bar stopped wiping his beer mug and looked up at the giant of a man. "Nobody hunts the Hunter anymore. He's killed over a hundred men, the Indians say he's possessed by demons and cannot be killed."

Duke leaned in close on the bartender, keeping direct eye contact. "Oh, he can be killed all right. You just point me in the right direction."

The bartender involuntarily took a half-step backward, "I've seen eyes like yours before... You're a Montgomery?"

"That's right. Name's Duke Montgomery and Richard Montgomery was my little brother."

"The Indian fighter from the West," said the bartender. "I served your brother many times, and he had many political connections here in Tallahassee. He was a man to be respected."

"Yeah, well, I'm a man to be feared," Duke said with a low growl.

Some cowhands closest to Duke overheard this and slowly stepped back from the busy bar and left the building. Duke watched their movement. This put a gap between him and the next set of patrons at the bar, he stared at them but they paid him no mind, so he went back to his questioning.

"So you can confirm that this half-breed killed Richard Montgomery?"

"Yes, Mister Duke, about a year ago. There have been many stories by men coming through here, from some that were there when it happened. It's known as the Big Lake Massacre round these parts. A year before that there were lots of men killed in Myakka City by the same half-breed; damn near burned the whole town to the ground."

Duke was becoming angrier by the minute. He slammed back another shot of whiskey to calm his nerves; the barkeep poured him another.

"Where is the half-breed now?" Duke asked plainly.

"No one knows fer sure, they say he went south deep into the swamps where no white man has ever lived, and not even the crackers will go there. His last known location was at Richard Montgomery's big house on the east side of lake Okeechobee."

Duke pulled a map from the back of his waistband and unfolded it, then placed it on the counter. "Mark the spot for this big house," he demanded by jamming his index finger with a tapping motion on the paper.

"I have no ink here. There's the bank down the street and to the south of town, or the hotel across the way has a quill." The bartender offered this nervously for he did not wish to say no to this man, but he truly had nothing behind the bar to write with.

Montgomery looked around the busy saloon 'til he spotted what he sought. At one of the tables sat an Indian dressed in a blue Union jacket with the sleeves cut off, suggesting he worked for the Army as a guide and tracker. An osprey feather stuck out of an armband wrapped around his bicep. With four large strides, Duke was at the Injun's side and plucked the feather from the band. As he did so, the man tried to stand up.

He only got halfway before Duke bent his trunk of a leg and kicked the man in the side, sending him and his chair flying across the room and to the floor. Duke took two more strides and stood in front of the Indian, waiting for him to get to his feet. The Injun slowly stood with one hand on his knife handle, his anger growing as he saw his feather in the big man's teeth. The Indian was clearly enraged but fearful at the same time as this muscle-bound giant loomed over him.

By this time, most everyone in the saloon had passed the word that this man was Duke Montgomery, the Indian fighter. But the Indian quickly decided he must fight to save his honor and pulled his ten-inch blade.

Duke grinned big, the feather still clenched in his teeth. With his right hand, he pulled one of his knives from his belt, leaving the revolver to hang in its holster. The Indian came at him cautiously, for he knew if this big man got a hold of him, it was over. Duke closed the gap with two steps and their knives *clacked* and *clanged* rapidly, like swords.

The observing patrons stepped aside as Duke forced the Injun back, one step at a time. The Indian knew his opponent's skills were superior, so he took a chance and pushed the point of his weapon forward in desperation. Duke moved to the side then grabbed his opponent's wrist with his free hand. In three quick blows, his blade came down in the same spot on the elbow joint, separating the Indian's forearm from his body—blood spurting out in all directions.

The Indian went to his knees, growling with pain, and then fell slowly to the floor as he bled out. Montgomery slid the Bowie knife back in his belt, crisscrossing it with the other, and took the Indian's forearm with him back to the bar.

The bartender stood there, eyes showing disbelief as Duke held the severed limb over the bar; a pool of blood forming as it dripped from the arm. Duke threw it to the floor, took the feather from between his teeth, and offered it to the barkeep. With a shaky hand, he took the quill and dipped it into the puddle of blood. The barkeep made an X on the map at the location of Montgomery's big house by the shore of the great lake.

"There, that weren't so hard now was it?" Duke said as he broke out with laughter. He picked up the map and held it out to the bartender and made a little puffing motion with his lips. The man behind the bar blew through his handlebar mustache on the bloody X until it was dry. Satisfied it would not smear, Duke folded the map and put it away.

Negro workers had dragged the body out and were busy scrubbing the floor as the saloon business went back to somewhat normal. They whispered of what just happened amongst themselves, but did not look too long in the Indian fighter's direction. Duke snatched up the half-empty bottle and headed for the door. Men and women parted, giving the giant man with dried blood covering his bare muscular chest plenty of room to pass.

As soon as the swinging doors came to rest, Billy and Junior followed. They left their table and pushed the doors aside as they exited. Three other men from the back of the saloon followed them out, also wearing red lambskin coverings over their shins.

The tension eased in the saloon after the Indian fighter and the others left the building. A man at the center of the bar got the bartender's attention with a nod of his head. Armed and clearly a rugged sort, he was the normal type of bad man who drank there, but nothing like the wicked Montgomery, or the hated red-legs.

"What can I git yah?"

"More whiskey," said the man.

"You can fill this one too," spoke a younger man who stood next to the other. His voice had a noticeable high pitch to it, forcing the barkeep to give him a second glance as he filled both glasses.

"That'll be two bits," said the man behind the bar.

The older of the two slid his two bits across the wood, "I thought I heard you call that big man Montgomery...any relation to Richard Montgomery?"

The well-dressed man behind the bar with the handlebar mustache said nothing, just continued drying beer mugs with the dirty rag.

The man slid two more bits across the wood, adding to the two that paid for the whiskey.

The bartender leaned in closer to the two patrons, so not to be overheard. "That was Duke Montgomery, Indian fighter from out West, the older brother of Richard Montgomery."

"I didn't know Montgomery had a brother." The younger skinny man spoke up, "What's he doin' here, anyhow? I heard they never found no bodies, so he ain't here for no funeral."

"True," continued the bartender. "Washington sent a small company to investigate, after two of Montgomery's men escaped and told their story. But all they found were two old squatters and a Chinese at the big house. No proof of a battle, and no bodies were found."

"He's here looking for the half-breed, ain't he?" the older of the two men replied.

"You know what, I'm done here," said the bartender as he slid two of the four bits back across the wood. "This talk never took place." The server walked away down the back of the long bar, waiting on other thirsty patrons bellowing for refills.

"What you think, Bodie?" the skinny young man asked.

"I think we owe the gunslinger. We need to find him and warn 'em."

"We don't even know where he is."

"No, but I'll bet Duke is headed for the big house. We got to git to Walt and Jebidiah before he does. If anyone knows where the gunslinger is, they would."

"What about our gold, Bodie?"

"We got the rig we need for that, Bird, and it's on that away. Sometimes you got to pay your debts before thinkin' of yourself. Now let's go, we got some hard ridin' ahead a' us."

Bodie and Bird left the saloon for their horses. They were already packed for the trail, and they had an advantage over Montgomery. They knew the land, being crackers born and bred in the south of Florida. As they rode out of town, they glanced to their right to see Duke Montgomery in front of the bank of Tallahassee dropping coins into the hands of five men dressed all in blue with red coverings over their legs.

The last thing they saw as they glanced to their left was a wood coffin leaning at an angle against a post. The undertaker tossed the severed arm on top of the Injun's body before closing the lid. The sound of nails being hammered faded as they rode south toward Lake Okeechobee and out of town.

Chapter Six

Hunter awoke from a dream an hour before the sun. He laid there, his open eyes staring at the many stars that lit up the clear black sky. Helen had rolled over out of his grasp during the night and her back was facing him, he could see her body moving slightly from her labored breathing as she slept. The crickets and swamp bugs were buzzing, and from the lake, the gators and frogs croaked their sounds.

Hunter watched a low flying owl searching for his next meal as he lay there, trying to remember his dream. After some thought, he recalled the eyes of the man he sensed was coming. The man was closer now and moving south, but that was all he could remember. Hunter's deep thoughts were interrupted by the sense he was being watched; he turned to Helen, who was now awake and looking at him.

"Are you seein' the man in your dreams?" she asked.

"Yeah, a little" Hunter answered, "but somehow his spirit image is dodgin' my recollection."

"Who is he?" Helen asked.

"I don't know him, but I *knew* him – hell I don't know. It don't matter anyhow, 'cause he's comin' this way and we're headed that way. Our paths must meet, so we'll find out soon enough." Hunter stood and collected his guns from where they lay upon the ground and strapped them on. "We need to git movin."

Helen jumped up and prepared for travel as Hunter buried the fire by kicking dirt over it with slides of his boot. They mounted their horses and headed north along the southern tip of Lake Okeechobee as the sun began to rise. The night creatures went quiet as the day animals came to life in their constant search for food. Largemouth bass, crappie, and blue gill hit shiners and bugs at the top of the water, making ripples in the morning light. Many ospreys and a pair of bald eagles flew over the lake searching for fish in between flocks of rival seagulls.

Hunter and Helen kept their distance from the rim of the lake, for the bank was where gators liked to bathe in the sun. An alligator getting hold of one of the horse's legs was unlikely, but a spooked horse could throw a man off his mount. Breaking a leg out here in the swampy wilderness could be a death sentence.

Early on, they ate jerky and drank water from a deerskin canteen for their morning meal. After a smoke, they rode hard for many hours.

By mid-afternoon, they had made good time and walked the horses to cool them down. Hunter turned them toward the lake, glad to get his sore butt out of the saddle for a time. They approached the bank cautiously, searching the ground for gators and snakes. He spotted a head with a pair of eyes jutting from the water, but the gator was small and out of reach.

The horses went straight to the water's edge, bowed their heads, and began to drink. Hunter and Helen continued to walk around, stretching their legs for a time, and then Hunter went through a check of his guns starting with his Colt .44 revolvers. There was no need for this, for they had been checked and cleaned after the last time they were shot, but old gunslinger habits die hard. Helen did the same, checking her Dragoons to find them loaded and ready as she had expected.

"We should reach the big house by this time tomorrow," Hunter spoke as he checked the sawed-off shotgun and then his Yellow boy rifle. He had just slid the rifle back into the scabbard on Zeke's saddle when both of the horses' heads came straight up and their ears went straight back.

Helen pulled both her pistols and backed up next to Hunter where he stood at the water's edge looking inland, toward the woods.

"What is it, Indians?" Helen whispered.

Hunter grabbed the Appaloosa's reins and handed them to her. "Mount up on Girlie and hold onto Zeke."

Helen holstered her guns and quickly climbed into the saddle. There was suddenly a crash just inside the woods, followed by an unpleasant odor.

Helen put her hand over her nose, "What is that, a bear?"

"A bear don't smell like that," Hunter replied.

There was another crash of trees then a series of wood on wood knocking sounds.

"Wait here." The half-breed walked across the small clearing and went to one knee at the edge of the tree line, his steel blue eyes seemed to glow with intensity. He stuck two fingers in the mud and marked his face with two lines down his right cheek; he dug more mud and did the same with the left cheek. The pungent smell had faded a little as Hunter thought he saw movement through the thicket. And then came a fierce roar. The half-breed stood and with two steps vanished into the woods.

The roar spooked the horses, and they were giving Helen a fit, but she managed to calm them down. She had the horses turned with their backs to the lake and nowhere to go; she had one pistol pulled and aimed at the woods, and the other hand held the reins of both animals.

Hunter did not have to go far to find the source of the crashing sounds. Two downed pine trees looked to have been pushed over out of the ground, their roots sticking up disturbing the forest floor. It would have taken an enormous amount of strength to do, for pine tree roots grow deep. The smell like wet air still lingered, but was diminishing.

Hunter moved deeper into the woods where he found a large branch that had been torn from one of the downed pines. It was lying next to a larger tree with its bark missing where the sound of the wood on wood knocks had seemingly come from. Whatever had been here was gone. Hunter could see the path it had taken as it left and the urge to follow and find out what creature could do this was strong. But he had no time for this, for he had a different kind of monster to find, a human one. Hunter had turned to head back, when he stepped down into an impression in the mud. The half-breed looked down to see he was standing in a footprint; twice as long as his boot and half again as wide, amazingly with imprints of five large toes at its front.

The horses had calmed down completely, but Helen had not. She was on full alert and had wrapped Zeke's reins around her saddle horn, freeing up her hands so she could hold both revolvers which she now aimed in the direction of the trees. When she heard the snap of a branch coming from the woods, she immediately cocked the hammers back on her mini Dragoons. A tense moment passed before Hunter appeared out of the thicket.

Helen let out a sigh of relief and lowered her pistols, "I didn't think that was you comin'. You're always amazingly silent when you walk through the woods."

"I was making noise on purpose not to startle you and git myself shot."

"What the hell was out there?" she asked.

"You wouldn't believe me if I told yah," he replied as he unwrapped Zeke's reins from the saddle horn.

"Try me."

Hunter looked into her eyes as if pondering whether he should say anything, then after a short pause...

"The Creek Indians tell a story of a creature that stands nine feet tall, and gives off a pungent odor. The Creeks and the Seminoles call it *Wettapo*, which means broad or wide; the Crackers in these parts call it 'The Skunk Ape'."

"I agree with Skunk Ape," said Helen. "That was the worst scent I ever smelled."

Hunter mounted up and took a last look through the trees past the clearing.

"Let's move, lady. We got three hours or so before sundown, and I don't want to be anywhere around here when dark sets in."

"I'm with yah, Mister, but wait a minute." She rode up next to him and wiped the mud streaks from his face. He allowed it and she then leaned forward and gave him a passionate kiss on the lips.

"Don't git me started," he said with a wink. They rode off, keeping closer to the rim of the lake, not as worried about the reptiles any longer, but more troubled about what might be lurking in the inland woods.

Chapter Seven

Jebidiah, Walt, and the Chinese cook named Chin-Yang had lived in Montgomery's stilt house since after the battle where Richard Montgomery and many of his men were killed over one year ago.

Those dead bodies were dropped into the gator pit under the house, leaving little trace other than a mangled hat or boot. Afterward, Jeb and Walt shot the gators under the house. They prepared the meat for food and used the skins, claws, and teeth for jewelry, clothing, and trade. They removed the fence that kept the gators under the house and the trap door in the first floor room was boarded up, leaving no trace it had ever been.

They spent months patching and fixing the house, covering up all signs of the battle that took place. Wood planks with bullet holes were replaced and the fire damage on the first floor had been repaired. For the first six months, Jebidiah and Walt had to deal with newspaper reporters and some Federal investigators, but the only evidence of the war between Richard Montgomery and the half-breed were stories and rumor.

The old coots told their story over and over again, and stuck to it. The land the big house was set upon was not deeded, so the old men claimed it for their own under squatter rights. They downplayed any battle that was rumored to take place, and when Chin-Yang was questioned, he suddenly did not speak English.

The visits by the newspapermen, Union regiments, the curious, and the passersby soon turned the big house on Lake Okeechobee into a profitable trading post, eatery, and hotel-saloon. They even had steamboats, commercial and private, docking for passengers and supplies from time to time. With the travelers came information, men traveling for weeks on end with stories from place to place came pouring out like the whiskey that flowed from their bottles.

Walt and Jebidiah felt fortunate that their time left on this earth was short as they knew times were changing. Clearly, the North was going to win the Civil War and the future of the South was uncertain. What concerned the old hunters this late morning was some news told to them by very reliable sources. Bodie and Bird had arrived late the previous night, their horses exhausted and close to death. After their morning meal, the four men sat at a table on the second floor discussing their mutual problem.

Bodie voiced to them about Duke Montgomery and his actions at the Tallahassee saloon, and what they were told by the man behind the bar.

"You got to be shittin' me," Walt said with disbelief. "We got another devil seed Montgomery to deal with?"

"The barkeep was convinced," Bodie replied. "I didn't see the Indian fighter's eyes but he did, and the barkeep knew Richard. Either way, it matters not who he is or ain't, 'cause he's headed this way."

Jeb sighed, "I need a drink." He stood and went to a cabinet, opened it, and returned with two mason jars, one filled with clear liquid and the other colored yellow. Walt had left the table and returned with four shot glasses. Jeb poured while he spoke, "Since it's early, we'll start with Apple pie."

They all slammed back their shots as Jeb remained standing so he could refill their glasses around the table.

"I knew Richard better than most," continued Bodie. "He was a hard man, but this Duke is worse than that. This one's pure evil, whether he's a Montgomery or not makes no difference."

"And he's comin' here for sure?" Walt asked.

"Yes sir," said Bird, "and he's got five red-legs ridin' with him."

"I'm a gittin' way too old for more of this shit," Walt replied, as he slammed back another shot. He slid his empty glass over to Jeb, who was now seated. "I'm ready for some of 'dat Okeechobee."

Jebidiah opened the jar with the clear liquid and poured into Walt's glass. Then he slid it back to him while he spoke, "So we got the meanest Indian fighter west of the Mississippi, which just happens to be the older brother of the man we killed and then fed his body to the gators, comin' here with a small army of red-legs. Is that what you're sayin', Bode?"

"He's comin' for the half-breed."

Walt broke into the conversation, "So, what are we worrin' fer? We just tell the same story we been tellin' for a year now."

"He knows this is his brother's house," said Bodie. "At the least, he'll throw you two outta' here. My guess, he'll kill everyone here and burn this place to the ground."

Chin-Yang entered the room and stood in front of the men at the table and began to speak, "Mister Trenton Bodie correct. I know of Mister Duke for many years. He is evil. He kill my son for spilling soup on his boot; he slit his throat with big knife without thought. Mister Richard said nothing, they continued to eat. Duke reached in his pocket and slid payment over to Mister Richard for dead slave. When he comes, I will hide. He is a dragon in human form – can only be killed by a chosen one."

Bodie and Bird looked to Jebidiah and Walt who just shrugged, not knowing how to reply as Chin-Yang had his say and then left the room.

"I don't know about all that, but it don't sound none too good," Jebidiah replied.

"For the year I know'd him, that's the most I heard that Chinese speak," Walt said, surprised.

"Where's the gunslinger?" Bodie asked, while raising his hands up.

"Hadn't heard hide nor hair," replied Walt, "Not since him and Helen went south and deep into the swamp."

"Then me and Bird will head south and try to find him. He must be warned, we owe him that much."

"We'll be goin' with yah," said Jeb while he looked to Walt. Walt nodded his head in agreement, then Jeb continued, "If there's gonna' be a revenge war, there's no one better to have on your side than the Half-breed gunslinger." They all nodded their heads, admitting this to be the truth.

The sun had been up nearly two hours and they already finished the Apple pie and then began work on the Okeechobee whiskey. Bodie and Bird always traveled light and could leave at a moment's notice, but Jebidiah and Walt would have to shut down and lock up the big house. They couldn't find Chin-Yang, his few belongings were gone and so was he.

Due to the lawlessness of the time and place, early on Walt and Jeb picked a spot not too far from the house and dug an underground bunker to hide anything of worth. Their shares of Richard's gold, furs, ammo, food, moonshine, and anything else they did not wish to be stolen were set in the wood-planked hole. They spent a few hours clearing out the post, filling the bunker to the top with the help of Bodie and Bird.

Bodie was the lookout, making sure no one witnessed the location of the hiding spot, while Bird helped with the loading. The rooms of the house for fee were empty, as the few trappers that showed for trade and food had moved on. Walt pulled the wood ladder out and slid the wood cover over the pit. He kicked dirt on the top, dragged a mess of palmetto palm fronds over it, and then raked away the footprints that led to the opening. Jebidiah chained the front door of the big house and pondered in his mind, questioning if they would ever see the place again.

The four men's saddlebags were packed, the horses watered and fed for travel. They gathered at the back of the house and were making last minute checks of weapons and tightening the saddle straps.

"Which a way we headed, Jebidiah?" asked Bodie.

"South, deep into the 'Glades, that's where we'll find the gunslinger."

"The Everglades? Can you narrow that down just a bit, maybe?"

"The last time we found him," Jeb continued as he stroked his white beard, "he was livin' on a lime rock island in the middle of nowhere; he may have gone back there."

"I sure hope you're right 'cause we're huntin' a needle in a haystack, for sure," Bodie commented.

Bird was already in the saddle and looking impatient, "Where's Walt run off to?" he asked.

"He's enjoyin' the outhouse one last time," Jeb answered.

"You damn right on that!" said Walt as he walked up and into the clearing. "Sure beats hangin' my backside over a downed tree trunk and searchin' for the softest pinecone."

This forced Jeb's jawline into a grin, Bodie shook his head with a short snicker, and Bird, being thirty years younger than Walt, found little humor. "Bunch a' old coots," he said irritably.

"Oh, quit your squawkin', there youngin', Walt shot back. "When you've hung your nekked tail-end out there on the trail as many times as I have, you'll git it."

Bird just rolled his eyes as the older men groaned while pulling themselves up into the saddle.

"Daylights a wastin'," stated Jebidiah as he led them South.

Walt tucked in behind him, then Bird, with Bodie bringing up the rear. Bodie was a strong, middle-aged man with the smarts of a leader, and his skills with a gun were quite good. Bird was young, but well trained by Bodie, and looking to prove himself.

Jebidiah and Walt were veterans of past wars, trackers and hunters second to none, and they had the experience only time can give. They were an assorted army, but they did have two things in common. They had heart and they all felt privileged to personally know the Half-breed Gunslinger who had become a Southern legend.

Chapter Eight

Duke Montgomery and his five hired guns rode out of Tallahassee just hours after Bodie and Bird had left the town. The difference in the speed the two parties traveled, put Duke and his men two days behind.

The red-legs had raped and pillaged southern families for pay and to feed their hatred for the rebels. But, their feelings were small compared to Montgomery's hate and urge to kill. Duke took what he wanted from whoever he chose. Florida had become the hideout of lawbreakers, renegade Indians, bushwhackers, draft dodgers, and anyone else not interested in choosing a side, North or South. So when these men were seen riding the trails, it surprised no one across these lands.

Duke and his followers were coming down a dirt road that split a field of sugar cane five feet high on both sides of the lane, with drainage ditches running alongside to their left and their right. Duke was always on point with his army of five red-legs following single file behind him. They came to a more narrow side road that turned deeper into the field and a medium-size cabin could be seen a half-mile from their position. Smoke billowed into the morning sky from the chimney.

Duke brought the quarter horse to a halt and looked around through the cane, and then down the road toward the cabin.

After a time, Billy came alongside his leader. "What is it, Sir?"

"We're being watched from the fields," Duke answered.

"How many you reckin'?" asked Billy, as he looked to the high stalks of sugar cane.

"Three, four maybe," Duke said as he leaned over and spit chaw juice to the ground.

"Have you seen them?"

"No, but they're there. Come on. Let's see if we can drum up some of that Southern hospitality I heard so much about." Duke turned toward the cabin and led his men down the road. As they got closer, Duke could see a man sitting in a rocking chair on the front porch. All was quiet except for the sounds of the horses' breath, the *clip-clop* of their hooves, along with the creaking of leather, and the clanking of metal.

The six men fanned out in a line in front of the cabin. No one spoke. The man on the porch was old and weathered, and was whittling a piece of wood, as he rocked back and forth. Duke noticed he had a single revolver tucked into his belt, but so far, the man paid them no mind.

"Old man," Duke said loudly, "I see the fire's a burnin'. You got any hot food inside?"

The elder did not reply and continued to scrape at the wood with his folding knife. His head was down and his worn hat covered his eyes, white stubble could be seen on his chin along with his white shoulder-length hair.

"Maybe he's deaf or dumb or somethin'? Junior commented.

Duke leaned around Billy toward Junior with a staring look, "Sorry, Duke, Sir." Junior said nervously.

Duke turned his attention to the cabin and took notice of the wood shutters closed over two windows. Pulleys at the top with a rope were used to swing them up and open from the inside. "Grandpa," Duke said, bringing his attention back to the old man, "maybe you know the whereabouts of a half-breed, goes by the name Hunter James Dolin?"

The old man suddenly stopped whittling and slowly raised his head. Making eye contact with Montgomery, he began to whistle *Dixie*. As he finished the first verse, the two wood shutters over the windows flew up. Gunfire sprayed from inside the cabin.

The red-legs pulled their weapons and fired back at the windows while trying to control their spooked animals. Smoke filled the air and the sound of shots fired echoed through the fields. As soon as the old man's lips hit the first couple of notes of the song *Dixie*, Duke slid off his horse. By the end of the verse, he thrust his twelve-inch blade deep into the old man's throat, even as the old Southerner struggled to pull his pistol hung up in his belt.

The shutters closed as quickly as they opened. While both sides were reloading, the Indian fighter kicked in the front door to the cabin, the pair of razor-sharp Sheffields clenched in his large fists. The candle-lit room lightened with the opened door. Two men wearing grey coats wildly slid bullets into cylinders, but they weren't fast enough. Duke tumble-rolled forward as one man fired. The two bullets missed high as the Indian fighter came up out of his roll to one knee. He thrust the knife in his right hand to the hilt in an upward motion between the lungs and the ribcage of the shooter.

The other man raised his pistol at the Duke's big bald head, and fired. In the nick of time, Duke pivoted on his knee, swinging the rebel's body between him and the bullet, which blew out the back of the dying man's head, spraying more blood throughout the cabin. Montgomery pushed the body up and forward with his great strength, using his knife handle still lodged in the man's gut. Forcing the shooter backward, Duke dropped the body, and thrust over the top with his left hand. His knife buried deep into the forehead of the second man, the tip of the steel piercing the inner skull wall.

Duke exhaled to blow the blood from his lips as it covered his face and chest. He waited for the man to stop moving before he pulled the Sheffield back out, allowing the man to slide down the wall to rest, one body in the lap of the other.

Billy and Junior came through the doorway with guns drawn. Duke turned on them, coming forward with his eyes blazing and his face and chest painted red.

"Easy Sir, it's us," Billy said, while taking an involuntary step backward and stepping into Junior.

Montgomery pushed past them and exited the cabin.

Billy and Junior walked over and examined the bloody bodies at the back wall with amazement.

"*Damn*, Billy..." Junior commented while shaking his head, "He took out two armed men with just them big knives of his – didn't even need to pull his pistols."

"I see that, Junior. We gotta' watch our butts with this one."

They left the cabin and met Duke outside where he was washing the blood from his face, chest, and arms in a rain barrel off the side of the house. Without a word, Duke walked back out front and Billy and Junior followed. Two soldiers were helping a third onto his horse; blood could be seen soaking his shirt.

"Sir, we need to git Jimbo to a doc," one of the red-legs reported.

The other man added, "I saw an office for doctorin' in that town down yonder, five miles back or so."

"There will be no goin' back," Duke stated plainly.

"But Sir, he's gut-shot. If he don't see a doc—"

Duke pulled his revolver and shot the man between the eyes. He fell off his horse to the ground. "There will be no goin' back," Duke repeated.

The men looked at one another, but said nothing as Montgomery walked to the porch and lit a lantern with a match from his pocket. He then threw it into the cabin. The sound of broken glass was followed by flame as the dry wood caught quickly.

"Let's move!" ordered Duke as he mounted up.

The men did the same, following him back up the dirt drive as the cabin was consumed in flames. When they hit the main road, they turned to the South and spurred the horses into a gallop, leaving a cloud of dust behind.

From the back end of the dust cloud, three Negro slaves walked onto the road from out of the sugar cane where they had witnessed the massacre that just set them free.

They only numbered five now, but the red-legs were not concerned about hunting the half-breed a man short. Not with the Indian fighter leading them. In their minds, Duke Montgomery would take care of Hunter James Dolin. Their jobs would be to watch his back for any friends the half-breed might be traveling with. The legend of the North would meet the legend of the South in a battle where the only result would be death.

Chapter Nine

Hunter and Helen traveled by day, and sometimes by night, only sleeping somewhere in the middle, five hours at a time. The closer Hunter got to the big house, the more his survival instincts rose from deep within him. They had been living in the Big Cypress Swamp for a year, with little or no confrontations. But he was being hunted like an animal now, and he could feel it.

His main concern was protecting Helen. Hunter knew first-hand how bad men would use loved ones to gain an edge over someone they were after. Hunter only knew he was being sought by someone by his dreams which told him so. He recognized the eyes of the bald giant in his forewarnings, but his mind would not allow the connection to be made, just yet.

It was early morning and the sun had just begun burning off the fog that crept off the top of the big lake, warming up and clearing the day. The woods suddenly looked familiar to the gunslinger, as they had not changed much in a year. He tugged on Zeke's reins bringing him to a halt.

"Helen," he said sternly, "stay here." They both dismounted.

Hunter removed his elk-skin Jacket with the long fringe, rolled it up, and then tied it to the horse's rig. Helen did the same with her coat and began going through the motions of checking her Dragoons; the clicking sounds of the revolvers were unmistakable.

"The big house is right through those trees," Hunter said, nodding in that direction while checking his Colts. The clicking sounds of the larger calibers were different than her Dragoons, but also unmistakable.

"I know where it is," Helen told him. "You brought me to the same spot where I waited with the spyglass when you and Jebidiah and Walt began your surge on Richard."

"Good, very good."

"Are you testing me, Hunter James?" Helen asked.

Hunter slid the shortened, double-barrel shotgun from the saddle's sheath and broke it, checking the shells. "Life is testing, I am training." Hunter pulled the spyglass from its holder and tossed it to Helen. He looked toward her, opened his steel-blue eyes wide, and spoke to her slowly and with conviction, "Stay, here! Please, stay here!"

Helen said nothing, just stared back at him.

"Are you hearing me?" he asked.

"You just be careful, and I'll watch your back," Helen replied as she slid open the telescope to its full length.

Hunter knew that was the best answer he was going to get from her, and he also knew if women always did what they were told, life would be less interesting. After a second thought, he put the shotgun in the top mount sheath on his saddle for the purpose of an easy grab, and then patted his hand on top while looking to Helen. She nodded her head in understanding.

The Half-breed Gunslinger silently made his way through the woods toward the Montgomery house. As he got within sight, he spotted five bareback Chickasaw ponies tied to the posts at the front. Hunter pulled one pistol and cocked the hammer as he crept up behind the ponies, putting his palm on one hindquarter to calm the animal.

He could hear the sounds of ransacking coming from the open door that had clearly been broken open. He holstered his weapon and pulled up one hoof of the near pony to check; it was unshod. He checked the markings painted on the animals, they were of different tribes. *Renegades,* came to Hunter's mind.

The gunslinger suddenly felt he was being watched from the woods. He turned and pulled both pistols with lightning speed, cocking the hammers back with his thumbs in one smooth motion. *Nothing there.* He stared at a spot in the woods from where he felt the eyes upon him, then winked.

"How does he do that?" Helen said quietly, as Hunter stared directly at her into her circular view through the scope. He then turned and walked to the front stairs, going up the steps while Helen followed him through the eyepiece. She watched him enter the house and vanish out of sight. Jerking the scope from her eye, she whispered, *"Damn!"*

Hunter crept into the dimly lit room. He saw the backs of three Injuns dressed partly in Union soldier clothing. They were ransacking the very same room where the gunslinger had killed Montgomery's men a year or so ago. They must have just arrived for the room had only a few crates which they were now rummaging through.

With his revolvers aimed at their backs, he glanced up the stairs to his left, looking for the other two before he spoke. "Are you findin' what you're lookin' for?"

All three froze for an instant, and then slowly turned their heads, looking over their shoulder to see who had the drop on them.

"Come on around slow," Hunter commanded. "It's way too early for back shootin'."

There were two Injuns, shoulder to shoulder, who had been digging through a box in the middle of the large room. The other was ten feet away, to Hunter's left, digging in another, with about fifteen feet between him and them. The closest two turned slow, and he could see they each had a single pistol in the front of their belts. The gunslinger read this with his eyes in fractions of seconds and was ready for any aggressive moves.

The bigger Indian to his left turned, and had a Tomahawk in his belt. Hunter followed his eyes to where he looked at a rifle leaned against the wall, just out of reach. The Indian looked back to the half-breed, making eye contact when he realized he had given away the location of his weapon.

Hunter brought his attention back to the two in front of him. "You will want to slide them pistols from your belt and drop 'em to the floor," Hunter said calmly. The room had an eerie silence about it as no one made a move for what seemed to be a very long time, telling Hunter they were not going to give up their weapons.

Hunter slowly released the hammers of his Colts with his thumbs and slid them back into their holsters.

"Say when."

As soon as the two Indians' hands touched the butts of their pistols, Hunter pulled both his revolvers with the speed of a rattlesnake strike and gunned them down. Two bullets each in the chest, their pistols never even made it out of their belts as they hit the ground. The gunslinger turned to the big Injun straightaway through the smoke-filled room, but he had not stirred. As the smoke cleared out through the open door, Hunter could see the Indian considering his next move. They both knew he could not get to the rifle before he was gunned down with Hunter's Colts drawn.

The renegade slowly pulled his tomahawk from his belt, grasping it tightly. His eyes glanced at the one in the half-breed's belt. Hunter holstered his pistols and tied them down without a word. He pulled the tomahawk that crisscrossed with the thirteen-inch bowie knife in his belt.

As soon as he dropped the head down and slid the twenty-inch handle into his clutched fist, the Injun lunged forward. He brought his hatchet down in an overhead motion, attempting to split the gunslinger's head right down the middle.

Hunter brought his weapon up and blocked the blow, the hard wood handles met with a *clank*. Hunter pushed back. The blades locked, only separating when the two men shoved off each other. With arms held high, the steel blades *clacked* and *clanked,* back and forth like swordplay – moving forward then moving back, like a dance.

Hunter dropped down, leveling the weapon and with a swing sliced deep into the big man's thigh. Then coming upright with a backswing, he caught nothing but air, sending him off balance and to one knee, putting his back to his enemy.

The big Injun knew he would bleed out soon from the gash in his leg. With a last ditch effort, he went for his rifle.

Hunter heard the *click* of the lever action Winchester from the corner of the room just out of his sight. Relying only on the sound, Hunter turned and threw the tomahawk in an overhand motion. He continued to roll forward all in one movement as the gun fired. The bullet pulled at the end of his long black hair as it ripped through it. He came out of his roll, pulling the right handed Colt and coming to rest on one knee, hammer back, aiming where he expected the renegade to be.

He did not fire, but slowly drew forward the strike with his thumb, and holstered the weapon. Breathing hard, he got to his feet and walked over to the back of the room. The Injun's legs were straight out the way he was seated, leaning against the wall. When Hunter removed his weapon from the man's forehead, the body slid down the wall sideways. The renegade's head came to rest in a pool of fresh blood.

Hunter reached down and grabbed a handful of the Indian's long black hair and wiped the thickening liquid from the tomahawk blade. He stood and slid the weapon back into the front of his belt and reloaded his Colts. There were five horses out front and only three dead men at his feet. He would follow the same path as when he had hunted Richard Montgomery and his men back in the day, by doing a room to room search of the house.

It felt like a dream as he began his climb up the stairs. Then his mild trance was broken when he heard gunfire coming from outside at the back of the house. *Helen?* He quickly turned and hurried out the front door then down the side of the big house toward the back, dread building inside him as he went. When he came around the corner of the structure, he almost tripped over a dead body. At the last minute, he jumped over it, keeping his feet.

"Where yah been, Mister?" Helen said from her saddle, pistols still drawn.

Hunter looked down at the two dead Indians with bullet holes in their chests and bent limbs that told of a fall. He looked up at the balcony of Helen's old room where the back door stood open.

"They tried to escape out the back, but they didn't git far," she continued, a sound of pride to her voice.

"What part of *Stay here* did you not git?"

Helen replied, adding a smile that cut Hunter's anger in half, "Now what kind a' gunfighter would I be if I didn't watch my partner's back?"

"Where's Zeke?" he asked, trying to ignore her boastful playfulness.

"He's just beyond those trees."

"Is he tied loose?" Hunter asked.

Helen nodded, while still pointing in the direction of the tree line.

Hunter whistled twice, and a whinny was heard right before the Appaloosa burst out through the brush and straight over to the gunslinger's side. He stroked the horse's velvet muzzle while pulling two sugar cubes from the saddlebag. He curled his palm upward to the horse's mouth, Zeke gobbled them up, and then rubbed his nose on Hunter's cheek. Hunter hugged and patted his neck, "Goood booy."

"Would you two like to be alone?" Helen asked with a smile and upward roll to her eyes.

Hunter grinned at her joke, but said nothing for he was pondering something, the same thing that Helen asked him next.

"Where are Jebidiah and Walt?

"Not here," the gunslinger replied. "The place was locked up tight before the renegades broke in. But I don't think they've been gone long. A day or two, maybe."

"Comin' in, I noticed some tracks that were headed out down yonder," she said. "Looked to be more than two horses, though."

Hunter mounted up. "Well, let's take a look."

They rode over to where Helen had seen the tracks. He read them as they went along slowly, his head hung low.

"That's a good eye there, lady. There are four sets of tracks here, single file, one on top of the other."

Helen smiled as she followed. "Is it Walt and Jeb?"

"Yup, sure enough, the same animals they had before."

"And the other two," Helen asked, "are they following, or are they travelin' along?"

"I'd say they are travelin' together. If they were trackin', they would follow off to one side, not on top in line."

"What do we do now?' she asked.

"We go after them."

"What about those dead bodies back there?" asked Helen, "Two died by my hand and I cannot in good conscience ride off and leave them lying there."

Hunter was afraid she would go there. "Helen, if you think I'm gonna' break my back burying those renegade bastards—"

She interrupted him sternly, "We can't just leave them rotting in Jebidiah and Walt's house, it's not Christian, and ... well, it's just plain rude."

Hunter let out a big sigh as he rubbed his forehead, for he knew he would not win this battle. "All right, but the best I can do is to drag the bodies into the swamp. I don't think God will mind them feeding the creatures of His earth."

Helen agreed half-heartedly, for she knew they were running out of time. They went back to the house and one at a time dragged the bodies back into the swamp. Helen did talk Hunter into cutting branches and covering them to keep the turkey buzzards at bay. A good idea, for the circling birds would draw attention by circling above, marking the big house like a map. With the job done, Hunter locked the house up tight before picking up Walt and Jebidiah's trail once again.

◆❖◆

They rode for a while without speaking. Hunter picked up the pace and then slowed down again, and then stopped, studying a certain set of the tracks. "I'll be damned." He said.

"What is it?" Helen asked.

"I weren't sure at first but this print shows it clear, the one hoof print is Bodie's horse. I'm sure of it."

"Bodie?' she asked, a little surprised. "Why would he come back here?"

"Not sure. The other tracks must be the kid's, what's his name?"

"Birdie," Helen answered.

"Yeah, Bodie and Bird boy," agreed Hunter. "They're movin' slow and headed further down the river. With all the rain last month, it will be hard to cross. We should catch 'em, two days by the afternoon, if they keep the pace. Come on, let's ride."

Girlie followed Zeke at a faster speed as they headed south in search of their old friends.

CHAPTER TEN

Duke Montgomery and the four red-legs were traveling southeast, keeping to dryer ground whenever they could. At times, they had to move more inland, around bogs and marshes. Duke cursed as they were forced to travel farther east instead of due south to avoid the swamps, taking much longer for them to reach their next stop. The best traveling was behind them now, which had been along cattle routes where wild grasses grew for miles on end.

Duke did not expect to find the half-breed gunslinger in Myakka City – that would be too easy – but he did hope to find someone who could point him in his direction. Friends would protect him and foes would not give up his whereabouts easily, out of fear or without a price, but Duke had his ways of making people talk. According to his map, they were within a week or two of reaching his little brother's home. Duke was feeling like a starved dog about to devour his next meal.

Montgomery and the four men were traveling a dirt road, that seemed to be going nowhere, when they came across two poles. One on each side of the road meant clearly they had once held a sign between them. Duke jumped down from his quarter horse and walked over to one of the post with the old flat wood plank still hanging from a chain. He pulled away the vines that covered the sign and turned it over to the side with writing on it. *Myakka City Pop 60*

The '6' had been scratched out with the point of a blade, leaving the population at '0'. Duke returned to his mount and moved his men forward to see what had become of the city of Myakka, the city where he had been told the war between Richard Montgomery and the Half-breed Gunslinger began.

They entered the run-down city single file, Duke leading the way. The men were tired and dirty from the long road, but they were now tall in the saddle and on alert as they looked to every hiding spot from the center of the town. Duke brought his men to a halt. The only sounds were the horses breathing and shifting the positions of their hooves.

The saloon was to their left and a trading post stood directly across the street and to their right; the only buildings left standing. There was a large pile of burnt planks farther up and to the right, now overgrown with weeds and vines. A burnt out barn was at their front, the walls gone. The steps that once led to the loft still stood, but ended in mid-air going to nowhere.

"Billy, you and Junior join me in the saloon," Duke ordered. "You two, check out the post and stay on alert. Ask about the half-breed, and if anyone gives you a hard time, lock 'em down and bring them to me."

The two red-legs at the back of the line dismounted and veered off, walking their animals toward the building where the sign simply read, *Trading Post.* Jack and Warren were well armed and well trained in the art of war. Duke had not bothered to ask their names, so 'you two' was what he called them. If they lived long enough, he might get around to learning what their mama had named them.

Duke, Billy, and Junior rode their horses over to the hitching post in front of the saloon and dismounted. They wrapped the reins around the long pole that had four horses already hitched there. Duke noticed the whips hung from the saddles before he entered the open door.

Duke had to duck his head a little to clear the top of the door jam. Billy was behind him and thought, *big son-of-a-gun*, as Montgomery's shoulders filled the doorway.

When Duke crossed the threshold and saw the looks given by the four men drinking at the center table, he knew there would be bloodshed before too long. But he needed information and decided he would hold back, at first. They bellied up to the bar and Montgomery smiled big as the bartender faced him from across the three-foot wide counter top.

"What'll you have?" asked the barkeep.

His southern twang irritated Duke, but with some effort, he managed to keep his smile big. "Whiskey; and a beer."

The rugged bartender set three shot glasses and a bottle on the bar. He turned to the keg and poured the glasses of beer, and then returned, sliding them to the patrons. "That'll be five bucks."

Duke pulled a ten dollar silver piece from his pocket and flipped it on the counter. The metal on wood sound it made as it spun to a stop brought on more attention from the cracker cowboys at the table. Duke made like he didn't notice them, but he was totally aware of their presence as he indulged in his drink.

"So tell me, barkeep—"

"The name's Roy," the man behind the bar corrected.

"Of course, Roy. I'm lookin' for an old friend of mine. His name is Hunter James Dolin – know where he might be?"

Roy looked to the two men by Duke's side. "You travel with red-legs, Mister. I don't think the half-breed could be your friend."

Patience was not Duke's strong point, and he was already weakening. He turned to the crackers at the table and made an announcement, "How 'bout you

Southern boys – you know where the half-breed might be?"

"We ain't tellin' you shit, Mister," said one from his seated position at the table.

Duke turned back to the barkeep, and without a word, pulled his pistol and shot the man at close range. The bloody red hole in the middle of his forehead formed just before he fell from sight behind the bar. The sound of chairs sliding on wood could be heard as the men at the table scrambled to their feet while drawing their weapons.

Billy and Junior had already fanned out from behind Duke, and were now firing their revolvers and moving forward. The cracker cowboys were some of the toughest men ever created, but they were at a disadvantage this day. They were unable to level their guns before they were hit with lead. All four men fell to the floor while their bullets missed the mark.

Billy and Junior had emptied their revolvers and were reloading.

Duke had not moved from his spot at the bar. He was just calmly drinking his beer as he watched. Two of the cracker cowboys were dead, but the other two were only wounded. Duke slammed back his beer and looked to the men who were trying to get to their feet and back into battle position.

One man made it to one knee and tried to level his revolver at Montgomery, but his wounded shoulder slowed him down.

Duke turned and sidestepped away from the bar to create a lane, pulled one twelve-inch knife from his belt, and threw it. The knife spun several times before finding a home in the cowboy's forehead, well before he could pull the trigger. When he fell forward, the hilt hit the floor and drove the blade farther into his brain from his dead weight.

The last man saw this and scrambled desperately for the back door. He didn't make it for Duke took four big strides while pulling his other knife from his belt. He then thrust it into the man's back, and through his heart. With one swift movement, he pulled it out as fast as it had went in, the man fell dead.

Duke turned to the cowboy lying face down and stuck his boot under the man's shoulder and rolled him over on his back.

"Damn" said Junior as he and Billy stood over the dead men, their guns drawn.

Duke eye-balled Junior, and then bent down, pulling his knife from the cowboy's skull which released the last of his blood.

"Damn!" escaped Junior's lips, yet again.

Duke eye-balled him once more before walking to the bar, holding his bloody knives in each hand. He set them on the counter and grabbed a bottle of whisky by its neck. Taking a swig before pouring some on the blades, he then took a rag from the counter and wiped each knife clean. He slid the Sheffields into his belt in their crisscross position and walked for the door. "Let's go, these men don't seem to want to talk."

Billy and Junior followed the Indian fighter outside where they met Jack and Warren in the middle of the street escorting a prisoner toward them. Duke towered over the captive as they stood face to face while the red-leg soldiers held him at gunpoint.

"He's the only one in there, Mr. Montgomery," announced Jack.

"Does he know anything?" Duke asked.

"We were gittin' around to it when we heard the gunfire, so we brought him out here."

"What's your name, old man?" asked Duke.

"Chuck Lamb, sir. I already told these men that the gunslinger I have not seen in over a year."

Duke took a step closer and looked down on the merchant. "You seem like a smart fella, for a Southerner. I am a serious man, so don't you hold out on me."

"No sir," replied Chuck. "I have stayed alive by minding my own business and keepin' my mouth shut over my many years, and I—"

Montgomery cut him off in mid-sentence, holding up his hand. "That will not work here, Mister Lamb. In fact, it's just the opposite. If you don't tell me everything I want to know, you will surely die slow."

The old man began talking, telling everything he knew about the battle between Richard Montgomery and Hunter James Dolin. He talked of the blown up hotel that set fire to the town, burning half of it to the ground. Most people thought the half-breed to be dead, for a time, until he showed a year later at Mat's saloon. He killed Scooter Johnson's hired gunmen before dropping Scooter head first into the gator pit. Chuck went on, telling what he had heard about the second battle at the Okeechobee Lake house, where Richard Montgomery was said to have been killed.

"Stop," said Duke. He had been pacing back and forth, spinning a twelve-inch knife in the palm of his large hand. Over and around the wrist, he did it without once looking, the speed sometimes blurring the knife. "You have told me some things I had not heard, Chuck. But none of this tells me what I need to know. Where is the half-breed son-of-a-dog that killed my little brother at now?"

The merchant was getting nervous, for Montgomery's manner was getting worse. "They went south, deep into the swamp." Chuck spoke quickly hoping to satisfy this dangerous man. "Some say beyond the Everglades and into Indian territory, known as Big Cypress. That's all I—"

"Wait, you said *they*?" Duke stopped pacing and spinning the knife, and he was now looking straight at the merchant.

"Richard Montgomery's woman – she went with the gunslinger. Some say on her own; others say by his hand – I'm not sure which."

Duke began to laugh, a loud evil laugh that went on longer than it should have. His red-leg crew began to laugh along with him. The merchant just looked at all of them, not sure what the hell was so funny. After a moment, the laughter died down.

Still grinning, Duke slid the blade back in his belt, "All right, Mister Lamb the merchant. You go back to your little store with my men. We're gonna' need supplies for our journey south, and I trust we'll git a really good discount?"

"Yes sir, Mr. Montgomery," Chuck said with much relief as he backed away slowly toward the trading post. "Whatever you need, free of charge."

Jack and Warren escorted the old man, still holding him at gunpoint.

"What now, Mister Duke," spoke Junior. "We still headin' for the lake house, or we goin' to that swamp?"

"Lake house first, dummy. Now we got another place to look, and we have an edge. Women are a weakness that most men have, one that I do not. Now, git your useless hides over to that post and help them load up supplies. We leave in an hour."

CHAPTER ELEVEN

Hunter James and Helen caught up with the boys, just like the gunslinger had said, two days and late afternoon breaking into early evening. They followed the tracks headed for the same swamp where Hunter once lived on a limestone island among the sawgrass.

The time they were wasting bothered Hunter, chasing one another's tails while someone was bearing down on him was not a good plan. In the back of his mind, he knew who the eyes belonged to he saw in his dreams. Something in him would not allow the thoughts to come forward as they could not be the eyes of the man hunting him, for he was already dead.

Hunter stopped the Appaloosa suddenly and sat there. Helen's horse stopped without command, for Girlie was used to following Zeke's lead. Helen rested one hand on her pistol while Hunter stared through the thickening forest. The trees were yellow and Australian pines with a mixture of Cypress that would soon take over the landscape as they went deeper into the swamp. Hunter could not see any movement or hear any sound, for the wind was at their back. But he sensed someone was there.

Helen came alongside him. "What is it?" she asked.

"There are men and horses up yonder, just under a mile, and they have settled for the night," Hunter told her.

"How do you know this from such a distance?" asked Helen, wonder in her voice.

"I'm the Half-breed Gunslinger; it's my job to know these things," he said with a slight grin.

"Are you making a joke?" She sounded surprised.

"How am I doin'?" he asked.

Keep workin' on it," she replied, with a grin of her own.

"Let's go," said Hunter in his more normal serious tone. "And move noisy. We don't want to sneak up on them and give the old coots a heart attack."

"Now that's funny," said Helen. "You're gittin' better."

They moved forward, steering the horses off the trail for the purpose of crunching leaves and twigs under hoof. Hunter kept his senses alert until Zeke began to grunt and sound out in short whinnies, as he too could sense Jebidiah, Walt, and their familiar animals.

The click of rifles and pistols could be heard as Hunter and Helen approached.

"Who goes there?" said a threatening voice.

"Take it easy, old man," said Hunter as they rode into the clearing. "Save your bullets for the bad guys."

"Well, if this here don't seem somewhat familiar," spoke Walt, as he lowered his weapon.

Helen jumped down from her mount and gave Walt a big hug as he tried to tip his hat. She ran over to Jebidiah and gave him a big squeeze, crushing his Stetson in hand between them. Bodie and Bird had removed their hats as well, "Such gentlemen out here in the wilderness," said a smiling Helen. "Relax men, I don't need to be fussed over."

"Howdy, Gunslinger," said Walt. He tossed him a lidded mason jar.

Hunter caught it upright with one hand from the back of the Appaloosa. "Okeechobee shine, I assume?"

"Better than sunshine," spoke Jeb.

"Damn sure better than the rain," finished Walt.

Hunter and Helen gladly joined the camp, settling in for the night around a small fire. They ate deer steaks from a doe Jeb and Walt had taken down days earlier along the trail. Afterward, they passed around mason jars and smoked cigars.

Bodie and Bird told Hunter and Helen the story of their meeting in the saloon with Duke Montgomery, known in the north as the Indian fighter. Hunter stared into the fire, listening intently while saying nothing, and showing no emotion. Helen, on the other hand, felt sickness creeping into her stomach, and becoming visible on her face with every word spoken.

"Richard Montgomery was a bad man," said Bodie. "But this man Duke, well, he is something else."

"I should have known it was him," Helen spoke up. "I never met Richards's brother, but they wrote back and forth to one another. Richard spoke of Duke to me only once, and I did sense respect. But I also remember thinkin' there was a little fear there, as well."

Bird spoke up when Helen finished, "He is the biggest man I had ever seen, but I ain't scared."

"Well, you best be a little scared, boy," Bodie replied with a fatherly tone.

No one talked for a time. They were all waiting to hear the gunslinger speak, interested to hear what he had to say, which he finally did.

"I won't be hunted like a dog in this life or any other," Hunter said, and then looked to Jeb and Walt. "Again, this is my fight, and the revenge that served me for so long is now bein' turned against me. No one here need die 'cause of my past mistakes."

Jeb stood with a groan and Walt followed with a louder one,

"We've been through this before, Hunter James," Jeb announced.

"The answer is still the same," Walt finished.

Jebidiah gave Walt a look that said *I'm talking here* before continuing, "I thought this shit was over, dead and buried, but as usual I were wrong."

"I won't argue with yah there, Jeb," Walt said, smiling at his old friend.

Jeb ignored him, which wasn't easy. "We're gonna' help you finish what we done started." Jeb and Walt stood there looking at the gunslinger as if to dare him to argue.

"Damned old fools," said Hunter, knowing he could not spoil the loyalty of these men.

Helen leaned against Hunter, realizing that quiet times like these would be far and in between as they moved forward toward this battle, and closing the gap between them and Montgomery.

"We're with yah, Gunslinger," said Bode. Bird nodded his head in agreement. "But I would feel better if we had us a plan?"

Hunter smiled at his friends with closed-mouth laughter, which he did not do often.

It caught the attention of everyone. Helen was close at his side, and she could feel the change in his manner.

"I don't see what's so damn funny?" Bird said, looking at the gunslinger and then around the fire to everyone else.

"I was just thinkin' of Mat," said Hunter. He always wished I had a plan instead of rushing in with guns a blazin'."

It was now Jeb and Walt's turn to laugh, for they had known Mat well. The others allowed the three to enjoy their memories for a moment, before Bodie broke in, "Well, Gunslinger, I agree with the man you speak of. Got any ideas?"

"From what we know, Duke is headed for Montgomery's stilt house. By now, it's most likely he already stopped in Myakka City seekin' information. I would like to get to the household first and lay in wait. Maybe set up a few traps. But gittin' there quick might be a problem. We had to go further than normal to find a shallow place to cross the river to find you all. It were as high as I ever seen it, from the rains last month. So our only choice is to ride hard and fast, as I see it."

"There might be another way," spoke Walt.

"What's that?" asked Hunter.

"I know a way over that river that could cut our trip down by a day, day and a half, maybe."

"Wait a minute," asked Jeb, "you don't mean the Stump?"

Walt nodded his head up and down at Jebidiah with a widening of his eyes.

"What's this stump?" asked Hunter, a look of confusion on his face.

"It's not just a what; it's a who," Jebidiah replied.

"Would someone tell me what the heck you all are talkin' about before the sun comes up," begged Bodie.

Jeb put his hand up toward Walt. "Go ahead, you tell 'em, it's your idear."

"They call him, Stumpy. He's a little person, like a midget or dwarf, and he built a bridge over the river that he guards and charges to pass."

"So we pay him to cross, what's the problem?" Bird asked.

"Well, it ain't that easy," said Walt. "He's a heavy drinker and he don't take kindly to just anyone crossin' his bridge. He guards it like a troll, and he carries the biggest shotgun I ever did see."

"Jeez, Walt," Jeb spoke up. "The shotgun's a long barrel, but it ain't any bigger than normal. It just looks that way 'cause he only stands about three foot nothin'." Jeb showed this by holding his hand out flat and waist high.

"Yeah, maybe." agreed Walt. "He might be short, but he must go 'bout two hundred pounds and then some, he's as wide as he is tall."

With some laughter, Helen broke in, not sure if the old coots weren't pulling their leg with this unbelievable tale. "So you're tellin' me, we got a drunkard, bridge buildin' midget with a bad attitude who would dare try to stop us from crossin. Is that what you're tellin' us?"

"Well, kinda. But he weren't much of a builder," replied Jeb. "If I recall, the bridge weren't that safe, but we did make it across, nevertheless."

"All right, Jeb, Walt," said Helen. "Tell me, what is a midget doin' playin' like a troll in the middle of the Florida swamp – can you explain that?"

"I swears, little Lady, this is a true story," continued Walt. "The tale goes he came down here with one of them there travelin' shows out a' Kentucky, I believe. But when he got drunk one night, he head-butted the ring master in the belly like a billy goat, right in the middle of a show. So they fired his little drunk butt on the spot and left him here when the show moved on. They say the fight was over the bearded lady. He's known for bein' creepy with the women folk."

Hunter spoke up next, "So you two have seen this bridge, and even crossed this bridge, and you know how to get there, right?"

Walt and Jebidiah both nodded their heads up and down in agreement.

Hunter continued, "Well, that's our plan, then. Git to the big house before Duke Montgomery."

"What about this little stump guy?" asked Bodie.

"Well, what does he like, besides the ladies?" asked Hunter, glancing at Helen, then directing his question to Walt and Jeb.

"Well, he makes acorn beer and drinks from dusk 'til dawn," said Walt.

"Chicken," spoke Jeb. "He eats nothin' but chicken, I do recall that, and he fries everythin' in lard."

"We leave at first light and head for the bridge, and I will deal with the midget, somehow." With this said by the gunslinger, they all settled down for the night. An owl hooted off in the distance, between the louder sounds from a Whippoorwill that was much closer to their camp.

Chapter Twelve

The race to Richard Montgomery's big house was on. Duke and his men were headed there, and Hunter and his gunslingers would soon be on their way. Hunter and his crew hoped the Stump man's bridge still stood, whether the midget was there or not. If they could not cross the river, it would place them days behind in reaching the stilt house on Lake Okeechobee.

Hunter was the first to wake, an hour before dawn, followed by Helen, whose training and connection to the gunslinger allowed her to sense his movement. They began striking camp which woke the others, also trained by years of conditioned living in dangerous places and sleeping with one eye open, always wary of critters, Indians, and bandits that would steal or even kill for a mere morsel of food.

Walt and Jebidiah led the way for they knew the whereabouts of the Stump man's bridge. Next in line was Helen, followed by Bird, and then Bodie taking up the rear. Hunter rode off by himself, telling them he would catch up shortly, for he had to secure some payment for the keeper of the bridge. Without question, Helen and the men went on ahead. Each one of them trusted the gunslinger with their lives and knew he would return. Walt led them up river toward the midget's lair.

Hunter guided Zeke through the thicket toward grounds where he had hunted in his youth. After a mile, the woods turned into prime land for what he sought. He dismounted, removing his fringed jacket before he grabbed his bow and a quiver of arrows lashed to the Appaloosa's saddle. He nocked one arrow and slung the leather holder over his head and shoulder to hang by its strap. His Indian blood seemed to come to the forefront as he silently stalked the woods for one of the smartest creatures that lived in the forest.

Hunter sensed it a split second before he heard it. He stopped behind a massive pine tree and went to one knee, avoiding the giant pinecones that littered the forest floor. "*Gobble, gobble, gobble, gobble ... gobble, gobble, gobble.*"

From around a large patch of palmettos came a large male, strutting with his feathers erect, in full bloom searching for a female. Hunter pulled back on the taut string and aimed for three seconds before he loosed the arrow. The arrow hit the turkey high in the collar and continued on, deep into the woods taking the head with it, but not before it stretched the foul's neck to its limit. The headless bird began flopping and rolling and running around, jumping four feet in the air and bouncing off a tree before landing in a patch of palmettos. The fanned leaves shook and then finally were still as the turkey's nerves stopped firing.

Hunter retrieved the big bird from the brush and carried it by its feet allowing the blood to drip as he went to search for his arrow. He took five steps and then stopped as he realized the woods had gone eerily silent. He sensed danger, followed by a musky stench; the same stench he and Helen had smelled by the lake days ago. Hunter turned quickly as the hair on his arms and neck stood up on end with a chill.

Leaving the search for the arrow, he ran back to Zeke who was clearly spooked, but was able to hold his footing. Hunter jumped on the horse's back still hanging on to the thirty-pound bird. Zeke took off through the brush without any command to do so.

Almost back to the trail, they heard a howl off in the distance, along with several wood knocks. As soon as they hit the clearing, the Appaloosa was able to hit full speed, which he did, almost throwing Hunter to the ground. Somehow, the gunslinger managed to stay on his mount and hold the bird for their getaway.

Hunter and Zeke caught up with the others. He passed Bodie and Birdie and squeezed ahead of Helen by tucking in behind Jeb. Hunter made plenty of noise during his approach giving Bodie and Bird time to hear and see that it was him. Zeke did his part by neighing to all.

Helen smiled at him as he passed, and he obliged her with a wink. Jeb and Walt turned their heads around to look at the approaching gunslinger without breaking stride. They began to chuckle when they saw the big turkey tied to his saddle, having a good idea what it might be for.

They rode with little talk for several hours, putting the sun just past noon. Walt put his hand high and balled it up into a fist to warn everyone behind him he was coming to a halt. The area had opened up, allowing the others to come alongside Walt on both sides on top of a ravine. Walt spoke up a bit for the noise of the river was loud as the water rushed quickly here. He pointed through the tops of the trees toward the sky. "Two streams of smoke down yonder, one to the left and one a little more to the right. The whiter smoke would be the still, the darker smoke would be the cooker."

"So you're sayin' the midget is still down there?" Jedidiah asked.

"I'm sayin' this is the place and someone is still there, whether it be Stumpy or not, we won't know 'til we ride down there."

Without another word spoken, the gunslinger reined Zeke slowly down the ravine toward the billows of smoke indicating the camp alongside the river. They all followed in his tracks, one at a time. After a while, the ground leveled out and the sound of the rushing river grew louder.

Hunter spotted the roughly built bridge. Being very narrow, the horses would have to be led across on foot, one at a time, but at a glance, it was likely they could make it. Under this side of the bridge was a small shack with boarded up windows and a four-foot high door. Black smoke poured out of a small stack from its roof. Behind was a lean-to covering a still which poured white smoke from its stack. Next to that was a wire pen with a dozen or more chickens, clucking and pecking at the ground.

Hunter stopped in the clearing in front of the house. The rest fanned their horses out in a line, side by side next to the gunslinger. The rooster in the pen set the alarm with a series of crows to alert the proprietor of the camp.

The little door flew open and out staggered the smallest man Hunter had ever seen. He could see why they called him Stumpy. No taller than four feet, he was just as wide with an unusually large head. From it grew a braided ponytail, the end hung a foot from the ground, and his arms and legs were too short for his fat body. In one hand, he held a mug of beer, and a chicken leg in the other. As soon as he saw them, he dropped both to the ground and grabbed a long barrel shotgun leaned against the outside of the building. He wildly pointed it at the gunslinger and his crew.

"Take it easy, Stumpy!" hollered Walt. "We mean you no harm, little feller. It's Walt and Jebidiah. We used your bridge a year back or so, you recollect?"

"You done went and made me spill my beer and chicken!" the midget exclaimed with a slur, as he looked down at the half-eaten bird leg that lay in the dirt.

Jeb spoke up quickly, "Take it easy, Stump, and don't let that short temper of yours get you killed."

Bird could not help but laugh. "I get it. He's got a *short* temper."

Stumpy swung the shotgun in Bird's direction and a scowl appeared on his unshaven face. "I ain't *short*, you beak-nose fool!"

Bird and Bodie slowly put their hands on the butts of their revolvers. Bird warned the little man, "Don't be pointin' them barrels at me, you drunk, chicken eatin' midget!"

Hunter broke in quickly, "Take it easy, everybody. I'm Hunter James Dolin. Me and my friends here just want to cross your bridge, for a price to be named by you."

Stumpy's eyes widened a little when he heard the gunslinger's name and he lowered the shotgun, but not all the way. He seemed to be pondering. When he spotted Helen, a creepy grin came across his face.

"Don't even think about it – the woman is off limits," said Hunter. "But I got somethin' here you might like..." Hunter untied the turkey from his saddle and tossed it to the little man.

Stumpy tried to catch the bird while hanging on to the big gun. But his little hands with short, fat fingers could not do both as the turkey hit him in the chest. With all this happening at once, he was thrown off his balance and his short bare feet could not hold him any longer. The gun hit the ground, then the turkey, followed by the little man. He fell flat on his back with his little arms and legs flailing around as he tried to rock his fat body front to back, and then side to side, trying to get back to his feet.

Helen put her hand to her mouth to hide her smile. Hunter's eyes widened with amazement at what he was seeing. Reminded him of a turtle laid on his back in the road. Bodie and Bird were flat cracking up, and Walt and Jeb were smiling with lowered head and rubbing their brows while looking a little embarrassed.

The midget finally managed to roll on his stomach and get to his feet. The problem when he did this was he ended up with his back to his visitors. Stumpy turned around, his eyes wide, looking scared at first. Then his fear turned to anger as Bodie and Bird could not stop laughing. He went for the shotgun.

Hunter pulled his pistol and cocked the hammer back with his thumb. "Just leave it."

The Stump changed direction and picked up the dirty chicken leg and faced them before tearing off a piece of meat with a jerk. He smiled at Helen with a wedge of chicken stuck in his teeth, practically raping her with his eyes.

"Like I said, the girl is goin' with us," Hunter reminded.

"You may cross my bridge for the turkey and a pistol, that's my final offer."

Hunter looked to Helen. She made a face, but pulled one of her baby Dragoons from her holster and held it up for the midget to see.

"Ain't big enough," said Stumpy.

Hunter could not believe the size of the chip on the shoulder this half-man carried. He reached in his saddlebag and pulled out a Colt .44 long barrel he had taken off a man who once tried him long ago. He tossed it to Stumpy.

The short man barely caught it and almost fell over once again doing it. He checked to see if the gun was loaded, then satisfied, he tucked it in his belt. The revolver was as long as one of the midget's arms.

This got more chuckles from Bird.

"You drive a hard bargain, little man," said the gunslinger.

"Well, this ain't my first rodeo, now is it?" replied the midget. He picked up his turkey, stuffed the chicken leg bone between his teeth, and waddled over to the foot of the bridge. With his little hands full, he fumbled around to pull a rusty key from his pocket. Refusing to set the turkey down, he struggled until he unlocked the chain that blocked the way. He then took several little steps over to his shack, and slammed the short, wide door behind him.

The wood and rope bridge was narrow and shaky, but rot had not set in. Hunter went first, moving quickly, and then Helen, followed by the others. They made it across with little incident.

When they reached the other side, they mounted up and prepared to move out. They looked back across the river to see Stumpy standing there, his oversize shotgun in one hand, a mug of acorn beer in the other, and the new pistol rested in his belt with the end of the barrel running past his knee.

"You're all right there, Stump! You give trolls a good name!" yelled Jeb, with a chuckle.

"Yeah, don't you belittle yourself!" yelled Walt, getting laughs from all but the gunslinger who just stared at the half-man with wonder.

Stumpy weren't real smart, but he knew they were laughing at him. He took a swig from his mug and spat at the ground as the Gunslinger and his friends rode away with purpose toward Lake Okeechobee.

Chapter Thirteen

Duke's red-legs loaded up supplies they needed from Chuck Lamb's trading post. They told stories and laughed with the man, as if he were a friend. Then they shot dead the keeper, as ordered by Duke Montgomery. No reason for it as Lamb had given them information and worked with them as they had asked. But it was in Duke's nature to kill, as it was for the men who followed him. Once again, Myakka City was a dead town with no one left alive. Only time would tell if others would move in and start over – for the town's reputation of being cursed continued. The Myakka Cemetery would now be the largest plot of land in what was once again a ghost town.

Duke was beginning to realize the half-breed he hunted was not a normal Injun. He was a legend in these parts and men feared him, just like people in the northwest feared 'Duke, the Indian fighter'. The Half-breed Gunslinger had killed his little brother Richard, who he knew to be one of the toughest men in any land. Duke had trained him and brought him up from childhood.

Revenge had been driving Duke, but now he had more of a reason to kill the half-breed. When he slayed Hunter, a legend of the Southern swamps, Duke the Indian fighter would be even greater and more famous across all parts of the country.

Montgomery and his men rode at a steady pace, but not too hard, for they would save their energy until they had an actual physical trail to follow. They finished the day making good time and set up camp on the north shore of Lake Okeechobee. From his seat at the fire, Billy drank coffee and sipped whiskey. Junior handed him a bowl of stew that he took with a nod.

"Would you like some stew, Mister Duke?" Junior asked.

"No." Duke said simply.

"I noticed you don't eat much," Billy commented.

Duke looked at Billy through the smoke from his cigar.

The man's stare put Billy slightly on edge.

"I never eat at night, only once a day, in the mornin'. You go to bed hungry, you don't sleep deep. Injun savages will sneak up on yah in the night and cut your throat without a second thought."

Billy stopped eating, letting the words sink in for a moment as he tried to put himself in the Indian fighter's boots. He could not. "We should reach the house in a day or two. Then what?" Billy asked.

His question got the attention of the others.

"Any a' you packin' a spyglass?" asked Montgomery.

"Yes Sir," spoke one red-leg Duke had still not yet bothered to place his name. "I got one in my duffel, Army issue."

"If the half-breed is there, I want to see him before he sees us. Then we will take action on what I see. Now, shut up and sleep for we ride at first light."

The night was unusually cold for the time of year, and the men broke out blankets for warmth. But not Duke. He slept in his daytime travel clothes, shirtless, with his boots on, and weapons in place.

Billy was smarter than most, and when he heard something that made sense to him, he would then adapt. He figured the more comfortable you were, the less aware you would be of your surroundings. So when Junior brought him a cover, he turned it down. But he wouldn't go as far as removing his shirt, the mosquitoes were too numerous in the swamp. Billy was amazed that Duke did not seem to notice the bugs. Maybe his tight, scarred, leathery skin was a bad feeding ground for the buzzing blood-suckers.

The men drifted off to sleep for much needed rest from the road. Their last thoughts of the night drifted with them as the critters of the swamp came alive. An owl hooted off in the distance, and gators and frogs grunted from the cattails on the lake. They would continue to do so, until the rising of the sun.

◆❖◆

On the south side of Lake Okeechobee, the same sounds of the night could be heard in the camp of the hunted. The gunslinger was the last to sleep, as he lay next to Helen. Walt and Jebidiah were snoring up a storm, staying in time with the croaking grunts of the frogs and gators coming off the big water. Bodie and Bird took first watch on separate sides of the camp's perimeter. Since they were the hunted, they didn't have the luxury of being content. They could not be sure where the Indian fighter and his hunting party might be, so they needed to be cautious.

Hunter wished he could fight this fight alone, but he knew his friends would not allow it. They were loyal and would follow him, regardless of his wishes. Most important was Helen. He would not make the same mistakes as he had in the past; he would keep her close, where he would at least have a chance to protect her. He had trained her well and only time would tell if she could stand up in battle.

Thoughts of Richard Montgomery and his first love, Lilith, went through his mind. He tried to tap into the revenge that served him well in the past. But with Helen at his side, he could not find his old hunger for vengeance. He would have to rely instead on the love he felt for Helen for his strength. The gunslinger finally drifted off into a light sleep, knowing he must kill the last of the Montgomery's, if any of them were to be free.

◆ ❖ ◆

There weren't a cloud in the sky as the early morning sun broke over the horizon, sending every kind of bird into flight. Both crews were on the move after their morning meal and the striking of the camps.

Hunter and his people ate jerky from the saddle, for the prey must remain a step ahead of the predator.

Duke and his boys ate cooked food, since Duke made his morning meal his only nourishment for the day.

Neither group knew where the other was at this time, but fate had them heading to the same place.

Hunter was leading the way as they reached a very familiar clearing. The same clearing, inside the wood line, where Helen waited for Hunter only days earlier, when he flushed the renegades from the house. The same clearing where a year ago she had watched with the spyglass while Hunter, Walt, and Jeb made their attack on Richard Montgomery and his men.

They rode in quiet and dismounted. Hunter pulled the scope from his saddlebag and found a spot to view the house through the trees. He scanned from different directions, saying nothing for some time, longer than Walt could stand.

"Well, what do you see?" asked Walt at a whisper.

"The front door has been broken into again, and there are bodies strewn about, but there is no movement," Hunter answered, while collapsing the scope to its shortest position.

"What do you mean, *again*?" asked Jebidiah.

"It's a long story for another time," Hunter replied.

He began checking his guns, as was his habit. The others did the same, one after the other.

"We ride in slow, guns drawn. If anyone is down there alive, they will be held up inside."

They made their way through the tree line and in little time reached the house. Lying on his back in the doorway was the body of a white man, his boots up, bottom half outside and upper half inside, his mid-section across the threshold. He had an arrow stuck in his chest. On the outside grounds, there lay three dead Indians and another body of a white man.

Walt and Jeb dismounted to get a better look. "Cracker cowboys," Jeb announced. "Locals, and them's Lower Creek renegades."

Walt was on one knee, looking to the ground at the tracks that told him a story. "The Crackers were here first, before the Injuns attacked." He looked to the sky to see buzzards circling overhead. "Body rot has just begun. So this happened last afternoon or evenin', at the latest. The turkey buzzards have only just now found 'em."

Hunter dismounted and walked to the front porch where he looked in through the doorway. The place had been ransacked once more, and he noticed that more things were missing, since the last time he was here. Signs of his battle with the Injuns were visible. Hunter returned to the grounds where Helen was holding the horses together, treating them with sugar cubes from her supplies.

"Someone got away with the goods, 'cause there ain't nothin' left on the first floor," said Hunter. He moved to where Walt and Jeb stood.

Bodie and Bird came from around the corner of the house at that moment. "Two shod horses left out of here recently, packin' heavy," announced Bodie.

"Looks like you old coots have done been robbed," said Hunter.

Jebidiah and Walt glanced at one another, grins on their faces. Bodie and Bird understood, but the gunslinger was a bit puzzled.

"Not to worry," said Walt, pointing in the direction of their secret underground storage. "All the good stuff is buried right over yonder." Unknown to Hunter, the first thing Walt had done when they rode into the yard was to check the ground with an eye out for any disturbance.

"We left enough supplies in the house locked up to keep 'em from snoopin' around the yard," spoke Jeb. "Seemed to have worked, or maybe the Injuns got here before them cowboys had a chance to look further."

"You got extra ammo in that bunker?" asked Hunter.

"Some .44 cartridges, shotgun shells, and two full belts for the Yellow boys, if my memory serves," Jeb answered while counting off on his fingers.

"Any dynamite?" asked the gunslinger.

"Oh, *shit!*" said Walt. "There goes the house."

"What are you fussin' about now, old man?" asked Bird, confused.

"I done seen firsthand what happens when this *son-of-a-gun* gits a hold of explosives. There usually ain't much left of nothin'."

Hunter ignored Walt and looked to Jeb for an answer.

"One box, 'bout six sticks, I think, more or less."

Hunter rubbed his chin in thought before he spoke, "Bodie, in the mornin', you and Bird ride north for a half a' day, stayin' off the main trails. Do not be seen, do not confront – just scout the area and git your butts back here. Hopefully, we'll have some time to set up some surprises."

"You got it," said Bodie. "But what about the rest of today? They could be comin' already."

"Make an hour sweep on the north perimeter. Just to make sure they're not already riding up our butt, while we raid the supplies these two got buried," Hunter replied.

With a nod, Bodie and Bird mounted up and headed north, cautiously looking for any sign of Montgomery and his red-legs.

Helen stepped in closer to where the men were conversing. "What can I do?" she asked.

"We need to eat, but no fire. We can't take the chance of smoke givin' us away."

"I can do that," replied Helen, "I'll feed and water the horses first, and then put together somethin' for us." Helen pointed to the sky, where the turkey buzzards were circling. "Hunter, we need to bury these men. They won't hold off much longer."

"No," said Hunter, "we leave the bodies right where they lay." Helen gave him a look, but Hunter continued speaking before she could argue. "When Montgomery and his men git here, they will observe from a distance, just like we did. If they see what we saw, they will come on in. We will be hid and git the drop on 'em."

"That's a good plan, Gunslinger," agreed Jebidiah, "If we can stay hid."

Walt shook his head in approval.

Helen agreed half-heartedly. She didn't like leaving the bodies to the buzzards, but she accepted it once she understood the plan. She hoped they would not have to wait too long.

Hunter knew of Helen's concern and that her faith required respect for the dead. But when men were at war, sometimes they must break the rules.

Walt, Jeb, and the gunslinger cleared the dirt and deadfall that covered the door to the underground storage. They pulled the planks up. Walt smiled big as the first thing he saw on the mound of supplies was a single jar of *liquid gold*. He popped the medal lever that secured the lid, and took a big chug of the Okeechobee whiskey.

"AHHH..." was the sound he made before handing it over to Jebidiah.

Jeb took a drink and then handed it to Hunter who took a smaller, but respectable sip.

"Sure lucky that jar just happened to be on top and easy to git at?" the gunslinger said, with doubt.

"Luck had nothin' to do with it," crowed Walt. "I figured if I ever made it back here alive, I would most likely need a drink."

"And how'd you figure that?" asked Hunter.

"'Cause he always needs a drink," Jeb replied, laughing.

While the boys drank and did their work, Helen fed and watered the horses. She removed the animals' riding gear and brushed them down one at a time, and then re-saddled them for a quick getaway. She had moved the horses to a clearing inside the tree line, keeping them hidden from the north. If Duke came from the south, the plan would fail, but from what they knew of the Indian fighter, his arrogance and impatience would bring him in from the shortest route. She left the horses and started the short walk to the house, hoping they would have time to prepare further before Montgomery arrived.

The men removed the supplies from the pit and carried the extra ammo, the box of dynamite, and some dried meat inside the house. They had to step over the body that still lay in the doorway.

Helen met them at the front porch on their way back out. She thought she caught a hint of stink coming from the body in the entryway.

"Bodie and Bird are back," spoke the gunslinger, while looking toward the tree line.

Jeb, Walt, and Helen looked to the woods, but saw and heard nothing. Five seconds went by and they began to doubt, but then they heard the snap of a stick under hoof as the men rode in from the north tree line.

Bodie and Bird stopped in front of the porch. Walt made eye contact and then tossed Bodie a jar of the shine which he caught, opened, and took a swig with a grateful nod. He handed it to Bird as he spoke, "We rode hard several miles north through the swamp grass, and then circled back. We took the road from there. Not a sign of 'em. We got at the least 'til this time tomorrow – if they stay to the path from the north. But there ain't no guarantee."

"Yep, that's the only thing for sure, no guarantees," said the gunslinger. "But we got a full day to get ready, I figure."

"Hell, we might have a month, for all we know," spoke Walt.

"No," said Hunter. "If revenge is driving this man, trust me, he will waste no time."

Bodie continued, "We did come across some tracks, though. Un-shod horses crossed the road into the swamp, 'bout two miles back."

"How many, you reckin?" Jebidiah asked.

Bodie looked to Bird for backup. "Fifteen, maybe twenty?"

Bird nodded his head in agreement, and then took another sip of whiskey that made his shoulders shiver before he passed it back to Bodie.

Helen suddenly realized what and who they were talking about. Anger began to creep up within her. She looked directly at the gunslinger, who avoided eye contact.

"Sam Jones, *son-of-a—*" blurted out Helen.

"Take it easy, please, woman," calmed Hunter.

"I told you I'm gonna' shoot those Injuns if they talk dishonorably around me a second time, seeing as no one else will."

Walt, Jeb, and the boys looked at one another with uncomfortable confusion. Bird was a younger man and didn't notice the hidden tension a man and a woman sometimes had. He spoke up as if this was normal talk to him. "You two know the Chief called Sam Jones?"

Helen glared at the boy.

Hunter spoke quickly, trying to steer his way off the eggshells he was suddenly walking on. "We run across him and his braves a ways back. We did some, uh...tradin.'"

"I don't mean to offend, Hunter James," said Walt. "But I don't trust that red chief. And what the heck are they doin' sneakin' around here anyhow, other than to raid our goods?"

"That may be the case, Walt," answered Hunter, "but those Creeks have another reason than thievin'. Superstition also drives their movements."

"*Lus-tee Manito Nak-nee,*" said Jeb.

"Yup," agreed Hunter. "They're watchin' all right. If I git killed, they believe my evil spirit will spread across their land. They're gitten ready, if that turns out to be the case."

"Or maybe they'll be a friend to yah, to keep yah living, Gunslinger," Bodie suggested.

"It'll be dark soon," said Helen, still clearly agitated. "I'm gonna' prepare some food." She stepped over the body in the doorway, glaring at Hunter as she passed. He did not look back, for his senses told him all he needed to know.

"She's full of spitfire, ain't she?" said Walt quietly, with a grin as he sucked down more whiskey.

"Take it easy on that Okeechobee, Walt. We may be here for a while?"

"Don't you fret, Mister Jeb. I spied some corn in the field not too far from here, and if these gunfights don't happen soon, I'll be firin' up some still cans."

"You two stay on alert," warned Hunter. "Have no doubt, he's a comin' and comin' with a vengeance."

There would be no fires or candle light this night, for fear of giving away their presence at the big house, in case Montgomery and his men moved in during the night. They would sleep in shifts, keeping a lookout 'til the morn. Hunter would send Bodie and Bird north at first light to scout once again for Duke and his red-leg hunting party. If there was time, the gunslinger would set some traps that might just give them an edge in the battle.

CHAPTER FOURTEEN

Duke Montgomery and his men were now just three days away from Richard's lake house. They had ridden steady for long hours, and Dukes eagerness for battle grew. The red-legs were willing, but the reality of the legend of the Half-breed Gunslinger was growing larger in their minds the further south they traveled into the Florida swamp.

Duke had hired five more men they come across in a small brew house along the trail. These outlaws were northern transplants, two of the men once worked for Richard Montgomery, and had survived the big lake massacre. They had seen the gunslinger's work first hand. They now rode at the front of the line with Duke, for they knew the way to the big house.

Duke sensed the fear these men felt when they spoke of the gunslinger, but the pay Duke offered was too much for them to refuse. More importantly to Duke was the talk of the woman. If he could capture her and hold her hostage, it would give him a huge advantage over the half-breed. But how would he draw her out?

Duke knew this man would not repeat his mistakes of the past and would keep the woman close by his side where he could protect her. Montgomery pondered this and decided if he could not get to the woman, he would do what had always served him best. Ride in and use his skills to kill everyone in his path.

The Indian fighter and his nine men set up camp as the evening set on the swamp. They would arrive at the lake house at mid-morn two days from now, not knowing if the place was still standing or occupied. Coming in from the north, Duke planned on spying with the scope from a distance. Depending on what he saw, he would then decide their next move. He would have to dig deep inside himself to proceed with caution for going slow was not in his nature. The revenge for the Montgomery name was swelling up inside him the closer he got to the resting place of his little brother.

◆❖◆

Hunter, Walt, Jebidiah, and Helen spent their morning preparing for battle, while Bodie and Bird made the same run they had the day before, to look for signs of Montgomery.

Hunter and Jebidiah dug out the ditch under the walkout that connected the dock to the front porch. This allowed the water to run freely once again, to refill the gator pit under the house. When this was done, Walt, Jeb, and Helen followed the gunslinger, stepping over the body in the doorway.

The dead man was beginning to spoil, forcing them to cover their noses as they went down the narrow hall to the large main room. Hunter opened the newly uncovered door in the floor by a rope handle. The new water could be seen still flooding in and rising rapidly.

As Helen looked down into the hole, memories of a bloody frenzy came roaring back, making her feel a little unsettled.

"And what are you gonna' do with that?" Helen asked Hunter directly, pointing to the water-filled pit.

"On watch last night, I saw several pairs of red eyes on the rim of the lake. Gave me an inkling that all I got to do is lure them to shore and poach me some gators."

"Even if you can do this without losing a limb, ain't it a little big-headed to think we can kill Duke Montgomery and his men? What if they kill us first? I don't want to end up down there," said Helen, her hands going to her hips.

Walt and Jebidiah looked to Hunter and then to Helen. Back and forth their heads turned, as they followed the conversation while not saying a word, unwilling to get in the middle of the talk, just yet.

"Yes, the gators will be helpful in gittin' rid of the bodies at the end, just like before. But I got another plan. We're gonna' remove the door and nail a rug over the pit. If we can draw a couple men in here, they step on the rug, and down they go."

Helen shivered a little, thinking about being eaten alive by an alligator, but she thought it could work.

Walt and Jebidiah agreed it was a good trap, but Jebidiah did point out one problem, "Killin' a big gator is hard enough – now you want to capture some alive, in the short amount of time we got?"

"Not me, us." Hunter replied.

Walt just shook his head and mumbled, "I'm gittin' too old for this shit."

They removed the door in the floor by pulling the nails from the hinges. Hunter suddenly raised his hand. "Shush!" Everyone froze and listened. "They're back," said Hunter.

"I don't hear nothin'?" questioned Walt.

"He ain't been wrong yet," replied Jebidiah.

Hunter left the room, with Helen right behind him, and on her heels followed Jeb and Walt. When they stepped out onto the porch, Bodie and Bird rode in at a walk then dismounted from their sweaty animals. They looked worn from the trail.

"Still nothin'," announced Bodie. "We rode the same trail as before and found no sign. Didn't see no new Indian tracks neither."

"That means we have this day, and maybe 'til noon the next day," spoke Hunter. "Bodie, you and Bird set up the roof with ammunition for rifles and load up on extra revolver cylinders, as many as you got. Jebidiah, Walt, you two will hold up on the first floor shootin' from the windows. Sooner or later they will git around to breaking in the front door. That's when you might git a chance to lure them to the pit; but don't wait for 'em too long. You two high tail it up the center stairway and meet Bodie and Bird up top. Me and Helen will be in the woods at the perimeter and come in on their backside. Well, that's my plan, any questions?"

"Sounds good to me," spoke Jebidiah. "If there's five or ten, it'll work, but if there's twenty or more, I don't think we can handle that many."

"Bodie and Bird will pick off as many as they can from the rooftop, thinnin' them out a bit," Hunter pointed out.

"You damn right we will!" Bird spouted off.

"What about the dynamite?" Walt asked.

"I'm not sure yet," replied Hunter. "The trees are no good for bang-sticks, but if there's a way to use 'em, I'll find it."

"Just don't blow us up in the process," Walt said. He furnished a jar of shine from inside his coat pocket.

Hunter ignored Walt's comment and then continued, directed toward Bodie and Bird. "When y'all are done settin' up the roof, meet me down by the lake."

"Well, I'm not goin' near that lake," said Helen. "I'll take care of your horses."

She took the reins from Bodie and Bird, and led the horses to the clearing for watering, brushing, and then re-saddling. The boys began setting up their areas, while Hunter went to the pile of supplies they'd dug out from the bunker and now sat to one side of the house.

He first opened the dynamite box and went through each piece, one by one, very carefully. All the sticks were old and three had loose fuses. The three best sticks would ride in his inside coat pocket, the others he tied together with a rawhide string he pulled from the same box they had been held in. He looked around the yard and not liking what he saw there, he stood then walked around the back. He spotted what he was searching for – a big scrub oak between the tree line and the house.

Pulling his bowie knife, Hunter stuck it into the tree with an overhand motion, then using it to pull himself up he placed the three bundled sticks of dynamite into the crook of the oak where the limbs branched out. The height would put the sticks a foot above a man's head if he were on horseback. The three giant branches would surely separate from the trunk and fall with the explosion. It would take only one hit from a bullet to set off the dynamite. With this done, Hunter grabbed two ropes from the supplies and headed for the lake to look for any gators on the bank taking advantage of the warmth of the sun.

Bodie and Bird had the two opposite corners of the roof set-up with water, jerky, and extra ammo along with a jar each of Walt's Okeechobee whiskey. They were ready for the battle they hoped would never come. They descended the spiral stairs in the middle of the house to the first floor, where they met Jebidiah and Walt who were just finishing their work.

"Where's the Gunslinger?" asked Bodie.

"I guess by now he's down by the lake doin' a little poachin'."

"What are you talkin' about, old man?" asked Birdie.

Walt gave the boy a look known as the *Evil Eye* for the 'old man' remark before he spoke, "That's right, y'all weren't back just yet," Walt pointed to the hole in the floor, "we got to help him fill this pit with live gators."

"What you say?" said Bodie.

"We gonna' put that rug over the pit and try to lure some of them scoundrel's to step on it, they fall in, and git et up, *chomp, chomp!*" explained Jeb, with a grin. "Come on, we best git down to the lake and see to it."

Walt cracked up with laughter when he saw the look on the boy's face as he stared into the pit. They filed out down the narrow hallway, Walt and Bird the last in line, and Walt was still laughing.

"Knock it off, old man! I ain't scared of no gators," Bird blurted out, while bowing up like a game rooster. This made Walt laugh even harder, 'til it echoed off the walls of the narrow hallway.

◆❖◆

Hunter had already lured two six-footers on shore with cow meat from the kitchen of the big house. The meat had been salted but set too long, and though not fit to be eaten by men, it made perfect gator bait. He had the two gators tied to a tree, like pets with rawhide wrapped around their snouts for holding their jaws shut.

He was now working a nasty ten-footer he'd lured up onto the bank with a piece of meat tied to the end of a rope. Hunter pulled the bait in quickly and untied it. Then he walked toward the gator, holding out the meat, dangling it from his hand, drawing the gator further up the bank. As he walked backward, the gator followed him. He carried a rope in the other hand with a loop tied on one end, and tucked in his belt he had a long piece of rawhide. As the gator snapped at the meat, Hunter pulled it away.

After he did this a few times, he threw the meat into the dirt further up the shore and to his side. The gator went for it and Hunter made his move. He flanked the reptile and jumped on his back. The gator whipped his massive tail as Hunter grabbed the back of his large head with both hands. He used all his weight, while straddling the body to hold the gator down.

The gator thrashed and bucked and snapped. Hunter timed the opening and closing of the jaws, and then quickly clamped his hands on both sides above the jaw, holding the mouth shut. He slid one hand to the tip of the snout, and with the other hand he pulled the rawhide from his belt, wrapped it around the closed jaws, and tied it shut. The big gator tried to roll to throw Hunter off his back, but the gunslinger controlled the animal and grabbed the cattle rope. He slipped the loop over the wide gator head, down to the neck, and then pulled it tight.

Jumping up, he pulled on the rope and tried to drag the gator further away from the water the reptile was now headed for. It became a full out, tug of war battle. Hunter was losing ground until Walt and Jeb were suddenly behind him, grabbing the rope, and helping him pull.

The three men finally wore out the ten-foot gator and managed to tie it to a tree. Hunter stood breathing hard while Jebidiah and Walt found a seat on a nearby tree trunk.

"Damn!" said Walt, catching his breath and coughing deep. He pulled a cigar butt from his lips, looked at it, and threw it to the dirt. "Waste of a good smoke."

"All right," said Jeb between breaths, "now what?"

"We grab them up and take them to the pit," replied Hunter.

Walt looked to Bodie and Bird and said, "Looks like you two are up."

Bodie and Bird looked at one another with doubt. "All right," said Bode, "Let's git this over with."

Bodie and Bird carried the six-footers one at a time up the walkway and into the house. They hung the gators tail first on the edge of the pit. With a jerk of the wrist, they cut the rawhide with a knife, and let the gator's weight slide him into the water.

Hunter had to help Bodie and Bird carry the ten-footer due to his weight and his thrashing around he continued, all the way through the house. They did finally manage to get the big gator into the pit without anyone getting seriously hurt. Hunter then fed the gators small pieces of meat. Getting them used to feeding this way, so if someone might fall through they would pounce. Bodie and Bird slid the floor rug over the gator pit, while Jebidiah tacked each corner down tight with a nail.

Walt rested on a chair, sipping on a jar of shine.

"Now don't anyone forgit 'bout this trap," ordered Jebidiah, as he glanced over at Walt.

"What the heck you lookin' at me fer?" Walt asked, an attitude clearly heard in his voice.

"I'm just sayin', when you drink that Okeechobee you wander sometimes."

Hunter broke in on the old men's banter before Walt got heated. "That's all I got for traps boys, and it's really gonna come down to we kill them before they kill us."

"I just wish we knew how many," spoke Bodie. "That's gonna' make a big difference on whether we survive this deal."

"The best we can tell, there's five of 'em we saw, plus the Indian fighter." Bird said.

"There's a good chance Montgomery picked up more men along the way," replied Hunter. "Plenty of men for hire between there and here who got no problem killin' for money."

Jebidiah asked Bodie, "I meant to ask yah, what where you two still doin' in Tallahassee? I thought with all that gold, you were movin' north and out of the state."

"Well," said Bodie as he scratched the side of his head and looked down, "we kinda' lost the gold, and a good horse to boot."

"What the heck you talkin' 'bout?" asked Walt.

"We were takin' a shortcut through the marsh, and we lost the pack horse in a swallow hole. Damn near went in ourselves."

Bird broke in on Bodie's talk, "The gold's still strapped to that horse carcass. I dove down after it, but it was too deep and too heavy. We had to leave it. I could git to it, but I need a block and tackle to hoist it up."

"That's some bad luck there," Walt said, followed by a loud burp.

Bird walked over to him with an irritated look, took the jar of shine from him, and then took a drink.

"Bird can git a hook or rope on it, cut it loose, and then we can crank it out," Bodie finished.

"It'll take me two or three dives," said Bird, "but I'm a good swimmer. I'll git it, fer sure."

"So you put off gittin' your gold to come back here and warn us 'bout Montgomery?" Hunter asked.

"We figured we owed yah, Gunslinger," Bodie answered. "Jeb and Walt too."

With a nod to Bodie and then Bird, the gunslinger moved the talk away from himself, "It'll be dark soon. Bodie, you and Bird set on the roof tonight, sleepin' in shifts, one man on the north, one on the south. Whoever's on the north side, be awake, for they'll most likely come from that way. Jeb and Walt will stay on the first floor. Me and Helen are gonna' stay to the woods at the outskirts with the horses to the south. I don't think they'll come in at night without spyin' us in the day first, but you never know."

"One more thing," said Walt, toward Hunter, "I know you were wantin' to keep things the same way around here, but that body in the doorway has got to go if I'm stayin' in here."

"Yeah, it's stinkin' pretty good," agreed Hunter. "All right, come on, we'll drag it out in the yard with the others, but leave the front door open."

The men agreed and put the cowboy's body in a position just off the porch. They then set off for their areas for the night while the sun began to set. Hunter found Helen by the horses at the clearing just past the tree line. He would close his eyes tonight, but he would not sleep much, maybe not at all, until he or the Indian fighter were dead.

CHAPTER FIFTEEN

Duke Montgomery woke his men much earlier than the sun and moved them out, eating their morning meal from the saddle. He wanted to reach the big stilt house before daybreak and be in position to spot the comings and goings of anyone in the area. Normally, the Indian fighter would ride in 'guns a' blazing'. But he had learned on this journey, the Half-breed Gunslinger was someone to approach with caution.

They came in from the north, riding the rim of the lake and stopped in a wooded area before the clearing to the house. Duke and the guide dismounted and made their way through the thicket, looking for a spot to observe the house through the spyglass. The rest of the men remained in the saddle, checking their weapons with little talk. Tension filled the air.

The guide decided on a place at the edge of the woods where he looked through the scope, panning left and right while leaning on the backside of a large pine tree. The sun began to rise, the rays of light blasted through the trees and off the water of the big lake.

"What do you see, man?" demanded Duke, his impatience clearly heard in his manner.

"We're too late. Something happened here; there's bodies – Injuns and cowboys – two, maybe three days."

"How do you know? Give me that thing," Duke said as he took the scope from the man with a yank.

"The turkey buzzards are feedin' on 'em. That's how I know," replied the guide. He stared at Duke, angrily, as the Indian fighter scanned the area.

Duke's eye closest to the guide was closed, giving the man a quick thought, *I could pull my gun right know and blow a hole in your big bald head!*

Duke suddenly lowered the scope, turned his head, and stared at the man with his evil eyes, "Did you say somethin' to me?"

"No – no Sir, I weren't sayin' nothin'.'"

Duke went back to spying while the guide stared at him with awe and fear, wondering if this man had just read his mind.

"There's someone in there. They've left the bodies to make us think they have gone," Duke said.

"How can you know that?" asked the man.

"The front door to the house is closed," replied Duke. He handed the scope back for him to take a look. "What thief closes the door behind him after he leaves with his hands full of stolen goods?"

"Makes sense," agreed the guide as he focused on the door. "But how do we know for sure?"

"Those men you're ridin' with – which ones don't you like so much?"

The guide looked at Duke, knowing what he meant to do. "There's two that ain't been ridin' with me for long. The other two have been with me for some time."

"Send the two of your pickin' in to look around. I'm gonna' watch from here and we'll see if there is anyone hiding inside there to flush out."

The guide nodded in agreement and left without saying a word. He headed back to the men with Duke's orders.

◆❖◆

Hunter woke with the sun breaking through the trees. He managed a bit of light sleep over the night, giving him just enough rest to refresh his senses. He stood from the oak tree he had been leaning against, but then stayed still, listening to the sounds of the swamp. Hearing nothing out of place, he went through the ritual of checking his weapons. Afterward, he pulled the scope and began scanning to the north beyond the house, then to the tree line to the east.

He settled in on the bodies now covered with turkey buzzards as they ripped the rotting flesh from the bellies of the dead men. It crossed Hunter's mind that the birds didn't care whether the men were red or white, to them they were all the same. The round shape of the scope's view panned past the house, stopped, changed direction, and panned back.

Settling on the front door, Hunter cursed, "Damned old fools!" He was staring at a closed front door. *There goes any sneak attack,* he thought. Hunter knew the smarts that Richard Montgomery held, and he figured Duke would hold the same, for bad men did not live long these days without a clever mind. At that moment, he saw movement from the north. Two men on horseback, riding in slow, their weapons pulled.

Helen came in behind Hunter. He smelled her even before he heard her approach, reminding him that he must keep her safe, at all cost.

"What's goin' on?' she asked as she checked her baby Dragoons and then slid them back into their holsters.

"Two men on horseback headed for the house." he answered.

"Are they red-legs? Is it Duke?"

"Not crackers, local transplants would be my guess." Hunter folded the scope and slid it into his inside jacket pocket. "I'm goin' down there, I need to git the drop on 'em, take 'em alive, and find out..." Suddenly, sounds of gunfire erupted. *"Shit!"*

"What is it?" asked Helen, even as she pulled both revolvers and cocked the hammers.

"Bodie and Bird – that's rifle fire from up high. Stay here, Helen, and watch the horses." Then he was gone, running toward the house.

Duke Montgomery watched it all unfold from his circular view through the spyglass from the north. He followed the two men from his camp as they rode into the yard of the big house. He watched as two men appeared on the rooftop with rifles. Duke's men fired back with their pistols, but were quickly killed. The advantage the men with rifles had from their high position meant the men on horseback down below had been no match at all.

Duke studied the men on the roof after moving his position several times. They were white men, positioned as if waiting for trouble. Duke guided the scope back to the ground were his men now lay dead. That's when he saw *him.* He came out of the woods with great speed, dressed in black except for his buckskinned fringed jacket. He had a .44 Colt Walker revolver in his grip. The Gunslinger knelt down, checking one man for a heartbeat, then looked up and in Duke's direction – right at him – as if he were looking down the barrel of his scope.

"Half-breed," the sneer escaped Duke's lips, and, "You know I'm here don't you?" Montgomery blinked. The Gunslinger was gone from his ring of sight. Duke turned and headed back into the thicket to where his men lay in wait.

Hunter knew they'd been flushed out. He sensed he was being watched and he knew in his bones it was Duke the Indian fighter. He must warn his friends held up in the stilt house. He went to the front porch and yelled through the doorway, "Jeb, Walt, I'm comin' in. Don't shoot."

Hunter walked through the front door to find himself staring down the barrel of Walt's shotgun and Jeb's revolver. They lowered their weapons when they saw the Gunslinger's piercing steel blue eyes. Both men felt immediate relief the half-breed was on their side and they did not have to go up against this man in battle.

"What the hell is goin' on out there?" asked Jebidiah.

"Two men rode in from the north and flushed us out. I should a' known Duke was as smart as Richard was. The good news is Bodie and Bird picked them off from above. But now Montgomery knows we're here. We lost our edge. Someone closed the front door and tipped them off." Hunter looked to the old men, seeking an account.

Jebidiah looked to Walt, Hunter then did the same.

"I had to piss," said Walt with a shrug of his shoulders. "It was cold when I got back so I shut the door, I was half asleep and weren't thinkin. Sorry, boys."

Jeb bowed his head and rubbed his eyes with his thumb and forefinger, "What do we do now, son?" he asked Hunter.

"Warn Bodie and Bird. Then move your stance to the other room and set up behind the gator pit. Whoever you can't shoot comin' in maybe will fall in. If you git overrun, retreat to the second floor, and then the roof. I got your back down here. If they git past me and set a fire, be ready to bail out, got it?"

"Yep" said Walt. "Didn't mean to shut the door," he muttered, embarrassed.

"Nothin' we can do about it now, just git'."

The old coots went down the hallway and into the pit room. Hunter poked his head out the front door, looking for snipers. Convinced no one was watching the door, he darted out and to safety, behind a large pine tree. He had to figure Duke was as smart as his brother Richard, or maybe smarter. If he knew of Helen, he might try to gain an edge.

Alarm began to come over him as he looked to the south. That feeling suddenly turned to panic when he heard gunfire erupt from the woods where Helen and the horses were held up.

♦❖♦

Helen was on full alert after Hunter left her alone at the tree line. Then the gunfire had begun. She kept one pistol drawn and cocked, looking to the direction of the house for what seemed to be a very long time. Suddenly, the horses warned her from behind. She turned quickly to see two men, one flanking her from the left and one from the right. Helen's training kicked in and, with her only thoughts being of survival, her body quickly answered.

She fired on one man with the drawn pistol while at the same time she pulled her left revolver from its holster Pulling the hammer back with her thumb, she squeezed the trigger. She cocked and then fired again with the right while pulling the hammer back with the left, squeezing the triggers, and hitting her targets.

The red-legs fired back, but with orders to capture and not to kill her, they missed her skinny arms and slender legs.

Helen's shots were kill shots, and she put the men to the dirt. She had emptied both revolvers, but continued to pull the hammers back, firing at them, her aim still on the fallen men. As the echoes of the gunfire quieted, she realized she was yelling, and only clicks came from her weapons.

Helen holstered one Dragoon while quickly reloading the other. She then holstered it, and then loaded the next full cylinder. As soon as she locked the lever in place, she felt a presence behind her – she spun and fired.

Luckily, Hunter was fast, as he turned to the side and jumped back a step – the bullet whizzed by his chin.

"Oh my God!" Helen exclaimed as she ran to him and wrapped her arms around his neck. "I almost killed you, my love. They came for me. I don't know how I – ah…" She looked down on the dead men and shuddered.

"Easy, my lady, you did good," Hunter told her, as he felt her shaking in his arms. "Your training kicked in, you embraced it, and now you have been battle tested."

Helen stepped back from him and walked over to one of the dead men. She looked at his face and wondered if he deserved to die by her hand. She pushed on the shoulder of the body with her boot.

The man's eyes opened and he grabbed the back of her ankle with a forceful grip. He brought his other arm up, still holding his pistol.

In one quick motion, Helen knelt down, putting her right knee on the man's chest. With her left hand, she grabbed the man's wrist, guiding the revolver straight up while her right hand pulled her boot knife. With a downward motion, she buried it in the man's neck up to the hilt. The grip on her ankle let loose, and with a gurgling sound, the man's eyes closed for the last time.

Helen's teeth clenched as she drew the knife from the man's neck. Blood sprayed her arm and shot up, splattering the right side of her face. She stood and turned to Hunter, who had pulled his pistol, watching her back.

"Well done, Gunslinger. You survived to fight another day," he said.

"What now?' she asked.

"You live with it," Hunter replied. "One word of advice, though – when you pull a blade from a man's jugular, step back quickly and to the side to avoid the spray."

He wiped the blood from her face with a gloved thumb. Their eyes locked and Hunter had an urge to kiss her. He shook the urge off, and said, "We have business at hand, Duke will attack soon, or maybe wait us out; I'm not sure which. From now on, you stay in my sight. I will not leave you again, until it is just me and him.”

She wrapped her arms around her man and gave him a big kiss. She let him go with a smile, and said. “Let’s kill them all and end this, Gunslinger.”

“Help me with these two red-legs,” said Hunter. “We’re gonna send them a message.”

They found the dead men’s horses tied deeper in the brush and brought them into the clearing at the tree line. They draped the bodies over the saddles, tied them down with rope, and led the horses across the yard to the north end of the house. The movement sent turkey buzzards scattering into flight off of the three-day-old bodies that released their stench into the air.

Helen had to put her hand to her nose as Hunter whistled twice like the whippoorwill. Bird looked over the edge of the roof, pointing his rifle at the Gunslinger and only turning the barrel away when he saw who it was.

“You and Bodie, cover us from the north side!” yelled Hunter, just loud enough for Bird to hear him from his position up top.

The younger man nodded and disappeared from sight. Hunter and Helen led the horses to the north side of the house and pointed them in the same direction the first two men rode in from. Hunter pulled his revolver and shot it into the air. Both horses took off at run. They would find the camp where Montgomery and the others were holed up.

Hunter looked up toward the top of the house. The brim of Bird and Bodie’s hats could be seen at the edge of the roof. Hunter whistled like the whippoorwill, forcing them to look down.

“All clear,” reported Bodie. “There’s no movement in any direction.”

“Keep an eye out. We have some work to do down here,” directed the Gunslinger.

Hunter and Helen fetched Walt and Jeb from the house. The four of them wrapped the remains of all the dead bodies in blankets that were strewn about. They dragged them from the front and the back of the house to the edge of the yard, into a pile for burning. The rot was not just unpleasant, but dangerous – there was always a risk of disease.

Walt teared up as Hunter lit the bodies on fire.

"What the hell you cryin' about?" Jebidiah demanded.

"I ain't cryin," replied Walt. "It's just ... Well, that was my last jar of shine he dumped to set that blaze, gosh darn it."

Jebidiah put his arm around Walt and gave him a tug before releasing him, "Well, old man, if we live through this, I'll help you make some more, and you can count on it."

"Thanks, Jeb. You is a good friend."

Helen made a cross with two sticks which she tied in the middle with rawhide and threw it on the flaming pile. She bowed her head, and her lips moved quietly in prayer. Even though they stood upwind from the smoke, the vile smell drifted and lingered from the burning pile. Helen backed away and stood next to Walt and Jebidiah. She looked around and did not see Hunter anywhere.

"Where'd he go?" she asked.

Before they could answer, Hunter came out of the woods from the direction of where the horses were corralled. He carried a whiskey bottle in each hand.

"Hot damn!" shouted Walt with a big smile.

Hunter tossed one bottle to Walt, "I'll warn yah, that's Elderberry wine, of my own makin'."

Walt pulled the cork and took a good swig, "AAHHH ... not bad Gunslinger, a little weak." He handed it to Jeb, who took a drink and then nodded in approval toward Hunter.

"Gunslinger!" came a shout from Bird at the top of the house. They all looked up, while going to the ready. "Bodie's got to use the outhouse, and I'm gonna' go stir-crazy if I don't git off this damn roof for a bit."

"Jeb, Walt, can you two take the roof for a while?" asked Hunter.

"Come on Walt, let's git," said Jebidiah with a smack from the back of his hand at Walt's belly. They waved to Bird and left Hunter and Helen as they walked for the front door of the house, glad to leave the bodies to burn on their own.

Chapter Sixteen

Montgomery had seen what he needed to by sacrificing two men. The *Half-breed* was there, the same savage that killed his little brother, and insulted his family's name.

A single gunshot rang out off in the distance, separated from the gunfire earlier. Duke's men were getting antsy. They had already lost the first two men and the two sent to kidnap the woman were long overdue. Duke knew he had to set these men to action soon, before they lost their nerve. He pulled some whiskey from his saddlebags and passed the liquid courage around to help wash down their meal.

Just as he did this, horses came running into the camp. Plates of food hit the ground as men pulled their pistols and raised their shotguns. They saw the bodies draped over the saddles. Some men grabbed the reins and settled the horses down as the others covered the woods from behind, stepping slightly out of the camp to cover the outskirts.

"What the hell, Montgomery?" said one that was inspecting the throat of the dead soldier. "That's four men down in only a few hours."

"I now know what I needed to know," Duke said, plainly showing no regret.

The four men searching the outskirts returned with their report. "I reckin' that lone gunshot we heard was to send the horses a runnin', but there ain't no one follerin'."

Duke could see the men relax a little, but fear of the Gunslinger still showed on their faces. The Indian fighter knew he had to nip this in the bud, and quickly, or by morning he would be the only one left in camp. Duke walked to his horse and pulled a leather satchel of gold coins from his saddlebag. He tossed it to Billy and spoke to the men, "Split that up evenly and there will be much more after this is over. When I have the *Half-breed's* scalp hangin' from my belt."

Duke knew that having gold in their pocket would be more convincing than just the promise of it. Greed was sometimes stronger than fear. Along with their pride stoked in whiskey, Duke would turn the men back into the warriors he needed, and he had a long rest of the day to do it.

"We attack tomorrow at first light," Duke ordered. "Kill them all, and show no mercy. But leave the *Half-breed* to me – I will take him alone."

This plan was fine with the men and it gave them more confidence. Not one of them was eager to face Hunter James Dolin. Duke's orders to avoid the gunslinger would give them an out. They could avoid him without being accused of being cowards.

Some men would sleep tonight while some would not, for one reason or another. Duke Montgomery would not sleep or eat, for he had found that an irritable, hungry man was unstable and more dangerous. He would get his nourishment from meanness and revenge, rather than food. But whiskey he would drink, for it seemed to make him nastier than usual.

◆❖◆

It was decided Walt and Jebidiah would remain on the roof while Bird and Bodie would take the first floor room with the gator pit down the hall from the front door. It made sense to switch – the younger men could scale the spiral staircase and escape to the roof quicker and easier than the older men. Hunter and

Helen would stay in the woods at the perimeter, but not to the south with the horses as before.

Hunter figured Montgomery and his men had flushed out that area. He decided to hide in the thicker brush behind the house to the east, Zeke and Girlie by their side. Hunter planned on fighting from the back of his horse, and he wanted Helen to have hers in case she had to run.

"Will they come soon? Will they come in the night?" Helen asked as they rested, leaned against a large pine tree shoulder to shoulder.

"I think they will come tomorrow at first light. They have already lost four men today and the rest will be spooked. It is hard for white men to fight in the dark, but we must be prepared for anything."

Helen snuggled up to Hunter, "I am gonna' nap for a little, I feel a little sickly."

"Are you all right?" Hunter asked.

"I'm fine, "she replied. "I just need rest."

Hunter kissed her forehead, and then went through the routine of checking his weapons. He had pulled a stone from his saddlebags earlier and began sharpening the tomahawk traded to him by Apayaka Hadjo, Chief of the Miccosukee. He sensed this weapon was given to him for a purpose and might hold some sort of native power. Whether this was true or not, Hunter knew the blade would serve him best razor sharp.

CHAPTER SEVENTEEN

The rest of that day and night was long for Hunter and his friends as they stayed on the lookout for an attack. Finally, daylight was close to breaking through the Florida swamp, and the birds and land animals of the bog would soon begin their day in their relentless search for food. Only men have other purposes in life, as they are driven by emotions more than instinct. The last stand of the Half-breed Gunslinger and the Montgomery clan would be decided in the wilderness, on a small plot of land on the east shores of Lake Okeechobee.

Zeke was the smartest horse Hunter had ever seen, and he proved it once again as he woke the gunslinger with a couple of hoof scrapes on the ground inches from his leg. Hunter rose to his feet, stirring Helen. She jumped up, grabbing the rifle, and loading the chamber by cocking it.

"It's time?" she asked.

Hunter mounted Zeke. "Helen, if anything happens to me and the boys and we look to be gittin' overrun, I want you to mount that cracker mare and ride on outta' here."

Hunter tied his hat down with the drawstring and moved out without waiting for her to reply. The first shots rang out.

Jebidiah and Walt were ready when three red-legs rode into the yard through the tree line from the north. They couldn't get a good shot off, for they were taking rifle fire from others in the woods. This allowed the three men on horseback to reach the front of the house.

As Walt and Jeb fired, they took fire, forcing them to dive behind the solid wood rail that bordered the roof. Hunter rode in from the east tree line and made it around to the front of the house, chasing down the last of the three men on horseback. There was a big gap between the last man and the two up front. Hunter pulled his Colt and shot the red-leg in the back of the head. The man fell to the ground as his horse ran on.

The gunslinger fired at the other two men who already dismounted on the run and disappeared through the doorway. Wood splintered around the wood jamb, and he heard the last man to make it inside yell out in pain. Hunter figured it was a flesh wound, most likely the back shoulder.

But Hunter did not follow. Bodie and Bird would have to handle them. He couldn't leave Helen out on the grounds alone. Hunter removed the spent cartridge and replaced it with another. Then he turned Zeke toward the back corner of the house. He heard gunfire begin inside the house as rifle fire continued from the roof. The crack of Winchesters echoed throughout the woods. Hunter and Zeke quickly came around the corner, his guns drawn, he steered the Appaloosa with commands from his legs and feet, something Zeke became accustomed to over many years.

Two cowboys entered the back yard at a gallop, firing up at Walt and Jeb, who were busily dodging and firing back into the woods. When the men saw the gunslinger come around the corner of the house, they directed their fire upon him, but to no avail. The gunslinger did not miss.

He steered Zeke to a gallop with his spurs, right down the middle of the approaching horses. They were twenty feet apart, their riders held a pistol in one hand and the reins in the other. Smoke filled the back yard and by the time they got ten feet from one another, the cowboys fell backward to the ground, one followed by the other.

Zeke and Hunter rode down the middle as their horses ran past and out of the yard. Hunter brought the Appaloosa to a halt, and whirled him around. He looked to the dead men whose only movement was blood draining from their bodies. The man on the right had taken a 44 slug to the upper chest and one in his neck. The man on the left took one in the chest and one in his left cheek.

Hunter quickly reloaded as he glanced around for more confrontation. The rifle fire from the woods had stopped. Walt and Jeb came to peek over the back side of the roof. Hunter looked up in their direction.

"Gunslinger!" yelled Jeb. "We seen Duke ridin' east, through the sawgrass, outside the trees." Jeb pointed toward where he'd seen Duke.

Dread hit Hunter like a sledge hammer – Montgomery was going for Helen. With his revolvers reloaded and holstered, Hunter put the spurs to Zeke. They headed for Helen's last position as fast as possible. He reached where he had left her but she was gone, and so was Girlie. Only the rifle was left, lying on the ground.

Hunter followed, reading the tracks. She had let out at a fast pace. *Good girl,* Hunter thought, and then a curse escaped his lips. Duke was chasing Helen, Hunter saw from the hoof prints coming in from the side to join hers. Hunter kicked Zeke into a run and took out down the path, as they were headed for the open marsh grasses of the swamp.

Helen was running for her life and as she looked back, her fear grew. Duke was gaining on her fast. They were at full speed, knocking down the knee-high grass while plunging through ankle-deep water. Helen knew Girlie couldn't outrun Duke's large quarter horse, and she couldn't see Hunter. She decided then to head for a limestone hammock coming up quick and slightly to her left. She thought she could hide on the small island wooded with cypress trees, palm trees, and palmetto bushes, allowing her to buy some time. The hammock was small and Duke would find her quickly, but not until she could dismount and prepare a last stand with her pistols.

To Hunter it seemed like hours – or days – but finally, he broke out of the woods to see the back of Duke and his horse, running at full speed through the marshy grassland. Water shot up in a frothy spray from the hoofs of his horse as he went. Hunter veered Zeke to the left, just enough to look around Duke. He could see Helen's water spray. She too was at full speed, up ahead of Montgomery, and he was gaining on her fast.

Now Hunter began gaining on Duke even faster. Hunter saw Helen heading straight for a clump of trees, and with his spurs digging in, he managed to get even more speed out of the faithful Appaloosa.

As Helen approached the hammock, she glanced back to see that Duke had almost caught up with her. He was only forty feet away, if that, and the island was sixty feet at her front. There was no time to hide before she would have to turn and fight. Suddenly to her shock, the trees on the hammock came *alive*.

Sam Jones, the Chief of the Misscokee, and his braves darted out of the brush on horseback, side by side – twenty strong – coming straight at her. By the time she pulled back on Girlie's reins, she'd shot through their line, just missing the Chief and his horse. She came to a halt and turned her mare to see the line of Indians meet up with Duke the Indian fighter, creating a wall between her and Montgomery.

Duke the Indian fighter could not believe what he was seeing. He brought his quarter horse to a halt, facing odds no man could survive. The Chief and his braves stopped ten feet in front of Montgomery, and then the Injuns enclosed him in a semi-circle. Duke pulled his pistols and cocked the hammers back with his thumbs, pointing them at the Chief. All twenty braves cocked the levers and pointed their rifles at Duke.

"All I want is the woman," announced Duke. "Give her to me, and I will let you live."

"The woman is not mine to give," said the Chief of the Misscokee. "*Lustee-Monito-Nak-a-nee* is the master of the female."

At that moment, the splashing sound of Zeke's hoofs sounded Hunter's arrival into the semi-circle of Indians pulling his pistols as he stopped. By the time the Gunslinger cocked the hammers and leveled them out, Duke had turned his horse to face him at a distance of ten feet.

The Indians closed the gap behind Hunter – surrounding Hunter and Duke by completing the large circle.

"The famous *Half-breed* Gunslinger of the swamp," sneered Duke, his pistols aiming at Hunter, arms bent at his waist. "Not how I pictured your death by my hand."

"Duke the Indian Fighter, killer from the north," replied Hunter, his Colt .44s positioned the same as Montgomery's. "Just another evil seed, spawned by the Montgomery family. The picture of your death will be the same as was the death of your brother Richard, by my hand."

Duke's eyes were ablaze with hate and revenge. He stared into Hunter's steel blue eyes that were fearless and showed the steady glow of boldness and finality. Without a word, Montgomery released the hammers and holstered his revolvers, and then he climbed down from his mount.

Hunter did the same. They unbuckled their gunbelts and fastened them over their saddle horns. Hunter removed his black hat and jacket, draping it over

Zeke's back. Duke had only his hat to remove, hooking it to his saddle. One, followed by the other, smacked the hindquarters of their animals, sending them out of the circle between the braves who made up what was now the boundaries of a fighting ring.

Helen rode up beside the Chief. "Kill him! Shoot the Indian fighter and end this right now, please."

"This will end here," replied Sam Jones. "The Spirits must choose the way the lands will be covered." As the Chief spoke, the wind began to blow hard from the west. "The bad spirits these men hold can only be sliced away with the blade."

Helen was not ready to see her man die; she went for the pistol on her right hip, but found the holster empty. She turned her head to see a brave with her Dragoons in his hands. Helen knew she had failed her man and, for now, she would have to trust in the skills of the Half-breed Gunslinger.

Duke pulled his twelve-inch Sheffield knives from his belt. They were facing up, held in his large fists powered by muscular forearms and massive biceps. Hunter pulled his thirteen-inch Bowie and the toma-hawk, the knife blade facing downward and the Indian hatchet up for an overhand attack.

They rushed forward, closing the gap quickly, their blows made a metallic sound as the blades struck one another in a blurry outbreak which seemed to go on and on and on. The two men backed away and circled in step to the left, and then in step to the right, both men looking for an opening in the other's defense. Again, they moved in on one another and the metal sounds echoed across the grassy marsh for a time.

Then, Duke made a move that caught Hunter by surprise. They were battling, in close, when Duke stepped backward and dropped both knives to the watery ground. With the speed of a rattlesnake, he grabbed Hunter's wrists and thrust forward with a head butt, knocking Hunter backward, blurring his vision, and forcing him to one knee. It would have been over for the gunslinger if they were fighting on dry land, but the ankle-deep water strewn with grass gave him time to clear his head.

Montgomery stepped back and squatted down, searching for where he thought his blades fell. He searched in the water with his hands, not wanting to take his eyes off the gunslinger. But he was forced to glance down to retrieve his knives, when he felt them. As he looked back up, he was caught in the face by Hunter's boot, knocking him on his back with a splash.

The half-breed was on him in an instant, the tomahawk coming down with an overhand motion in an effort to split his bald skull. Duke's speed brought his blade up and blocked the tomahawk where the handle and steel met, stopping the razor sharp blade a mere inch from his head.

Hunter jabbed his other hand forward, intending to pierce the neck with the Bowie knife, but Duke thrust his body upward making Hunter miss. Instead, the blade went through and out the back of Duke's bicep which held off the tomahawk.

The big man let out a yell, and then brought his other hand up and across, hitting Hunter in the side of the head with the hilt of the Sheffield, knocking him off. Hunter landed with a splash and rolled over once, getting quickly to his feet.

Duke rolled to the opposite direction and did the same. They faced one another at a distance of ten feet once again. Both were bleeding from knots on their foreheads from the head-butt, and Duke had blood dripping from the knife wound in his right arm. Hunter's right temple pulsed with pain from the blow that forced him to his rolling stance. The two men stared at one another, the only movement their heaving chests, thrusting in and out with each gasping breath.

An evil looking grin slowly crept onto Duke's face. He dropped one knife and slid his hand down into his boot, pulling out a derringer. As his arm came up toward the half-breed, Hunter pulled back the arm that held the tomahawk. He slung it forward in a short forearmed stroke. Duke leveled out the derringer and pulled the trigger, a split second before the Tomahawk struck.

The top of the blade sank into Duke's forehead and the bottom of the blade shattered teeth before coming to rest deep inside his face, filleting the left side of his nose. The eyes of the Indian fighter rolled back into his head and he fell dead with a final splash. The grassy water turned red with blood as it flowed from his head.

Hunter heard muffled yells and the yips and hollers of the Indian braves that encircled him as he looked upon the dead warrior Montgomery, and then everything went black.

CHAPTER EIGHTEEN

Three days passed before Hunter regained consciousness. He heard voices in the distance that slowly seemed to come closer, louder and clearer. He forced his eyes open to blurry vision. With several blinks, the fuzziness cleared and he found himself looking at Helen's beautiful image.

"Oh, thank God," she said, "can you hear me? Can you see me?"

Hunter opened his dry mouth to whisper, "Water..."

Helen left his sight for a moment, and then returned to drip water from her fingers into his mouth. He took it eagerly before falling back into a deep sleep.

Hunter awoke once more to loud talking that was very familiar. "You think you old coots could keep it down a bit and let a man die in peace over here?" insisted Hunter with a weak voice.

"You 're a tough *son-of-a-gun*, there, Hunter James," spoke Walt.

"Good to have you back, son," said Jebidiah. "It were hit or miss there for a while. Here, I got a present for yah." Jebidiah handed him his old Colt Walker.

Hunter took the pistol, but he was weak and the weapon was heavy, so he set it on the bed next to him.

"Why do you have this, Jeb?" Hunter asked.

"Bodie and Bird brought it back with them when they went to fetch the Doc. They found ol' Stumpy face down in the chicken coop, dead. He'd done choked on a turkey leg bone."

Helen walked in through the door, "All right you two, out!" she ordered. As they moved through the door, their fussing became quieter. Helen brought a glass of water to Hunter's lips. He drank some and then saw a man he didn't know come into his line of sight at his bedside. His mind instinctively went into alert mode, but calmed when he saw the man holding a medical bag.

"Hunter, this is Doc Holt. Bodie and Bird rode days to fetch him."

"Let's help him upright," said the Doc.

They pulled him into a sitting position on the bed, and Hunter felt a sharp, deep pain in his mid-section. Helen put a pillow behind him long ways for support. Hunter knew it was stuffed with chicken feathers from the smell.

"You took a bullet in the belly," said the Doc. "A small caliber at a short distance, but thankfully it missed any vital organs. Problem was, it went deep and it took some time to dig it out. You'll live, if infections don't set in – if so, there's nothin' anyone can do. Now I got to go, I got to check on a cattleman's wife on the way back. She's with child." With this said, the Doc headed for the door.

"Thanks, Doc," said the gunslinger.

The man stopped and looked back from the doorway. "Oh, don't thank me. Your two old friends was the ones that dug out the lead. If not, you'd a been dead by the time I got here. Good day." And then he was gone.

"I'll be damned," Hunter said. "I didn't know Jeb and Walt could do doctorin'?"

"They can't," said Helen. "They're just good with a knife, that's all. Now that you will live, we need to talk."

"I ain't out of the woods, yet," he replied, a mite suspicious at her tone. "You heard what the Doc said."

She sat on the side of the bed and took his hand into both of hers. "Well, you best git through this, 'cause I'm with child."

Hunter jerked up a little and winced as he turned to look at her. "Say what?"

"I am with child," she said again, with a smile.

"How do you know?"

"In case you haven't noticed, I *am* a woman, and we know these things."

"A son," he said, an unusual smile showing.

"Or a daughter," she reminded him. "Are you pleased?"

"Yes, I am pleased."

"You git some rest and I'll bring you some stew in a little while." She kissed him on the forehead and left the room, closing the door behind her.

Hunter James Dolin laid there with a smile on his face, pondering the thought of the family he'd always wanted – a beautiful wife, children, and a proper home.

His smile slowly faded and, just this once, he wished he was not so familiar with his body. He suddenly could feel the infection setting in, deep down inside his wound.

The End

ABOUT THE AUTHOR

Bret Lee Hart, a second generation Floridian, has spent the last twenty-five years in Marine construction; he is married and the father of two. His mother's maiden name is Emerson, as in Ralph Waldo, and on his father's side, Edgar Allen Poe can be found hanging on the family tree. With this bloodline of writers, and being named after Bret Harte from his western short stories, it was inevitable his imagination would find its way into print.

The *Half-Breed Gunslinger, Hunter James Dolin (Book II), Montgomery's Revenge (Book III), Wanted Dead (Book IV), and Wars End (Book V)* are the five books in this "cracker Western" series, as Bret calls them, and are available at major online book retailers.

The Fangslinger and the Preacher, Preacher Jack and the Fangslinger (Book II) are also available with many other adventures soon to be unleashed from this exciting storyteller's mind in various genres, including Fantasy and the Paranormal.

Follow Bret Lee Hart on Facebook:
https://facebook.com/bretleehart

OTHER WORKS AVAILABLE FROM
BRET LEE HART

✳ ✳ ✳ ✳ ✳

~ A Western action adventure, the first in
"The Half-Breed Gunslinger" *series ~*

In 1860 there was more open range cattle in Florida than in Texas and all the other states combined. It took a special breed of man to live there, and an even harder man to survive. Hunter James Dolin, half white and half Indian, was such a man. He was a gambler by trade and a gunslinger of necessity and attracted trouble wherever he traveled. But with his two Colt Walkers and bowie knife, he could handle almost anything.

Brief excerpt:
About ninety miles back and a few days earlier, in the crackerjack Saloon along the Withlacoochee River, Dolin's ace-high straight flush had beat one of the three outlaws' full house. He won fair and square – two ounces of gold and a just 'broke in' Henry rifle. These days that was more than reason enough to kill a man.

Hunter had felt the itch in his craw that warned him he'd out-stayed his welcome, and knew it was high time for him to leave this place. Without taking his eyes off the men at the poker table, Hunter had gathered up his winnings, while he spoke, "Thank you, Gentlemen. It's been a pleasure."

The man at the table to Hunter's left, the one who just lost his Henry rifle, had stood and replied angrily, "Do you think we're just gonna let you walk on out of here, half-breed?"

* * * * *

Spurred by revenge...
Gunfights and gold...
One man against the odds...

Hunter James Dolin survived the revenge war of Myakka City, Florida, by killing the men who raised their guns against him and his loved ones – all but one.

The Governor directed the Army to investigate, forcing the Half-Breed Gunslinger to seek refuge deep in the swamps of the Everglades.

Hunter James Dolin was content to live the rest of his life in solitude – 'til he was sought out and told of the whereabouts of the one that got away.

This would spark a new battle of revenge, overshadowed by the Civil War, but not soon forgotten by the people who inhabit the Florida swamplands.

Brief excerpt:
Scooter was swinging like a pendulum as very large Gators came up out of the water and snapped at the chicken, just out of reach of the man's head. Scooter was screaming again, as Hunter backed Zeke up a bit, putting his face and head closer to the teeth-laden jaws of the twelve-foot reptiles. The largest of the Gators stretched his neck up and snapped two pieces of chicken hanging down less than a foot from Scooter Johnson's head.

"PULL ME UP!!!! PULL ME UP!!!!" shrieked the dangling man. "I'm not the last – Montgomery's alive! *HE'S ALIVE, PLEASE!!!"*

Hunter urged the Appaloosa forward so the rope hanging over the branch moved with him, pulling Scooter up and out of reach of the Gator's bite.

"What do you mean, *he's alive?*" yelled Hunter. "I blowed him up in his own hotel."

* * * * *

~ A Western action adventure, the third in "The Half-Breed Gunslinger" series, set in Florida. Author Bret Lee Hart reminds us his state was once as wild as the West – and just as deadly. ~

Duke Montgomery is an Indian fighter – a hard-as-nails killer, plain and simple – who doesn't think twice about ambushing a man or killing him face-to-face. When he learns his brother Richard is dead, killed by the Half-Breed Gunslinger, Duke goes on the hunt.

To avoid trouble after his dealings with Richard Montgomery, Hunter James Dolin and the woman, Helen, travel deep into the Everglades to live in peace for a while. But, as is the way of the world, trouble soon comes looking for them.

How many will die as Montgomery seeks the Half-Breed Gunslinger to get revenge? And what surprises are in store for Hunter James Dolin?

Brief Excerpt:
"Where you headed, mister?" asked Billy.

"Myakka City is my first stop," replied Duke.

"Where's that at, Billy?" whispered Junior, leaning toward Billy.

"Not sure," said Billy, "Where's that city at, Mister? Maybe we could tag along with yah?"

There it was; Duke had just recruited these two easily with his larger mind. He grabbed the whiskey bottle by its neck, and with the other hand chugged the last of his beer then slammed the glass mug on the counter. "We leave tomorrow mornin' at sunup, meet me at the hotel. You will be paid if you do your jobs and don't git yourself killed." Duke turned and headed for the door, taking his whiskey bottle with him.

"What might our jobs be?" said Billy to his back.

The shirtless, scarred, muscle man stopped and turned after two steps. "We're going to Florida to kill a stinkin' half-breed."

Billy and Junior looked at one another and grinned with confidence that the job would be easy enough.

"What do your friends call you, Mister?" Junior asked.

"I don't have any friends, but you will call me Sir." Duke turned and walked out, leaving the saloon doors swinging behind him.

* * * * *

~ A Western action adventure, the forth in
"The Half-Breed Gunslinger" series, set in Florida.

While *The Half-Breed Gunslinger* fights for his life against infection from a gunshot wound, there are wanted posters being printed with his name and likeness. A $5,000 bounty on the head of Hunter James Dolin is more than enough money to attract men to the swamps of south Florida. The ending of the Civil War turns soldiers into bounty hunters as the North feels the need to cleanse the South, and men find ways to make a living.

The gunslinger's woman carries his child; Helen will need help from their close friends as her pregnancy progresses. Jebidiah and Walt will protect Helen at all costs with their experience and grit. Bodie and Bird, with their own skills, will be by their side in whatever comes their way. To their surprise, unexpected rivals come after the newly named Dolin Family.

Brief excerpt:
"What's goin' on, Hunter? Talk to me."

"Bounty hunter keeping track of our whereabouts." Helen's hand went to the butt of her gun. "Easy, woman; he's gone for now, but he will be back and with friends."

"What will we do?" she asked calmly.

"We can't stay here, it's too open. We could hold them off inside the cabin but for only so long; eventually they would burn us out. Myakka City is where our friends are; they will increase our numbers."

"Then we'll git little James, Alameda and Mocha and go to town at once."

"It ain't safe for the boy or you. I think maybe you should take little James and go with Alameda to the Seminole tribe lands..." Before he could finish, Helen was on her feet and shaking her head.

"I will not stay with that Sam Jones; Alameda can take little James and Mocha out there but I will go where you go." She turned and began walking up the bank to the cabin. "We best git packin'."

Hunter knew Helen meant to stand firm on her decision and there was nothing he could say to change her mind once she had made it. The boy would be safest with the tribe and Helen's skill with the gun would be handy. She had been battle tested and had killed without prejudice. She would be more dangerous now that she was a mother, like a mamma bear protecting her cub.

* * * * *

*~ A Western action adventure, the fifth in
"The Half-Breed Gunslinger" series, set in Florida.*

The three year Montgomery/ Dolin War was over, and not one family member named Montgomery was left alive. Hunter James Dolin had killed Richard Montgomery, his brother Duke Montgomery and their sister Jane Montgomery. The next man in line named Little Owl, for Chief of the Snake Clan of the Miccosukee, of the Seminole Indian Tribe was killed by the hand of the Half-Breed Gunslinger. Little Owl and his loyal braves were no more.

Myakka City and the James family had survived the last battle and Helen and little James were found alive at the waters' edge. Their current enemies were dead but Hunter was concerned about the wanted posters. There was no way to know how many had been printed and how far they had spread? The authors of the prints were dead but it would take time for this to be known and then believed. Five thousand dollars was a world of money and there would be men coming to kill the Half-breed Gunslinger and seeking their fortune.

Brief excerpt:
"The knife," said Hooker.

Hunter reached back and pulled the bowie from the sheath that was clipped to his pants at his back. Daryl took that too, with the same grin, only bigger.

"You take good care of that, Daryl; I will be needin' that back."

The stare of the gunslinger's steel blue eyes froze Daryl for a moment. His smile faded and then came back, but only a little.

"Oh, you won't need this no more, half-breed, not where you goin'."

"Daryl! I'm only gonna tell yah one more time to shut the hell up," the Captain warned. "Jimbo, tie his hands in the front; he's got to ride."

The big mouth drover picked up Hunter's pistol belt from the floor as Jimbo escorted the gunslinger outside. Zeke was there, and Hunter was placed on his back by two of the men.

"Where we headed, Captain?" Hunter asked.

"Daryl and Jimbo here will take you to Fort Foster and we'll let the army decide your fate."

"What of my family, Captain?" Hunter asked.

"When they are ready for travel I will personally escort them wherever they would like to go, unharmed. I give you my word as a lawman and a gentleman."

"You do as you say, Captain, and I will allow you to live. I give you my word, but your men here, a pass will not be givin'."

Jimbo glared at Hunter and Daryl laughed out loud.

"Let's go, tough guy," Jimbo replied.

"You try anythin', half-breed, and I'll kill yah with your own guns," Daryl said while resting his hand on Hunter's 44s that he now wore on his hip.

Hunter was glad to see his bowie knife tucked in the man's belt for he would need it as well on his return.

* * * * *

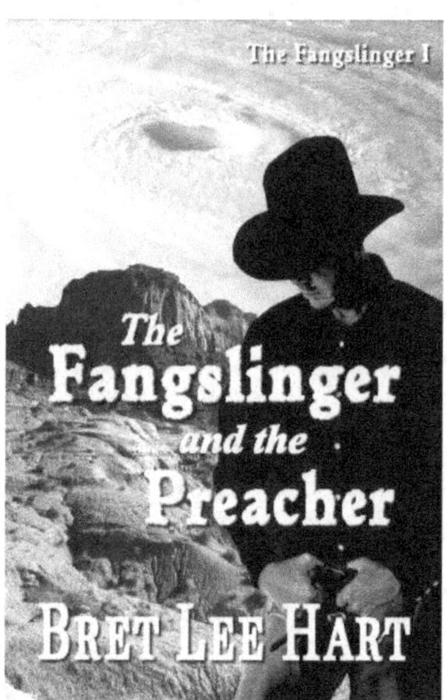

*~ A Paranormal Western based on the
age-old battle of good versus evil ~*

Master Andelko Balas is the leader of a bored, and therefore troublesome, vampire coven in Romania in the 1880s. Colonel Richard Andersson brings relief to the boredom by discovering tales of the American West and setting the coven on an exciting, but bloody, journey to a new land.

Jack Denton, reformed gunfighter, former preacher, now a drunkard, has visions of a great evil coming to Arizona as he wanders in the desert. Then he meets an Indian Chief and is given a silver sword, a special cross, and a mission. Jack is led to Black Mountain Mesa where an unusual storm is brewing and he has to face the greatest battle of his life.

Is this the last battle for the world as he knows it? Will his renewed faith and special weapons be enough to defeat such evil?

Brief Excerpt:
Black Mesa Mountain, Arizona, 1885
He went by the name Preacher Jack, given to him by his small congregation in New Mexico. He had buried the name Anderson in the past, going by the name Jack Denton in fear of being discovered by the law, or the lawless. It was a simple life he now led, and a good life for Preacher Jack, until God's plan for him continued forward. When his wife and daughter died from disease that swept through the small Mexican village, Jack lost his faith in God and left New Mexico, wandering aimlessly, not caring if he lived or died. Forty-year-old Jack Denton, a fallen preacher, was now a faithless drunkard living off whiskey – his only thoughts were of drinking himself to death.

Forty days and forty nights into his journey of despair, Jack found refuge in an abandoned mining shack to get some rest. A vision appeared to him as he slept, the drunken haze in which he slumbered left him, allowing the vivid images of his dream to come forth...

Fear overwhelmed him as something that Jack could only describe as a demon straight from hell swooped down on top of him, baring bloody fangs to devour his flesh.

Jack Denton awoke with a scream from the dirt floor of the mining shack.

✳ ✳ ✳ ✳ ✳

~ The Paranormal Western sequel to
"The Fangslinger and the Preacher" ~

Preacher Jack and his comrade Richard, a centuries-old Romanian soldier, thought their battle against evil was won after their climactic battle with the master vampire Andelko Balas at the top of Black Mountain Mesa. But Richard's former master was not vanquished permanently; the Fallen One has raised him up, and now Balas has an undead army at his command. The Preacher and the Fangslinger, aided by the mystical Indian White Owl and his followers, are now all that stands in the way of the vampire master's plan to empower his dark lord and unleash hell on earth.

Will the Preacher's faith be strong enough to sustain them?

Brief Excerpt:

On his return to camp, Jack was surprised to see that Richard had pulled himself up and was now leaning against a flat rock formation alongside the campsite that partially blocked the dry desert wind. As Jack got closer he could see that the color in Richard's face was much better. Jack then realized that the colonel had positioned himself in a shady spot to avoid the rays of the morning light. This concerned the Preacher, for this was something a man with the blood of a vampire might do.

"Does the sun bother you?" Jack asked.

"Slightly, yes," answered Richard, "may I bother you for some additional water?"

Jack fetched the canteen and went to one knee as he handed it over, but this time Jack did so at a greater distance.

Richard took several small sips, and then the two men stared at one another for a moment.

"You do not trust me so?"

"Ain't sure just yet," answered Jack, "you did save my life on that mountain, and the rumor is that we are kin, but the simple fact that you're hidin' from the sun does got me wonderin'."